Welcome Wagon

"So let me guess," Slocum said in a tired voice. "You want me to leave?"

"Oh, you'll be leaving all right. Feet first."

Both men stood side by side. They spread out and began stalking forward with cruel intentions written across their ugly faces.

"What's the meaning of this?" Slocum asked. "You gonna tell me what this is about?"

"You're John Slocum?"

"That's right."

"Then you should know damn well what this is about."

"How about you enlighten me?" When neither of the men responded, Slocum squared his shoulders to them and placed his hand less than two inches above his holstered .44. "If you want to steam ahead without explaining yourselves, that's fine by me. I can ask my questions to whoever shows up at your funeral."

That stopped both men dead in their tracks. They were well within the serviceable range of their shotguns, but didn't seem as keen to use them as they'd been only moments ago. The one who had been called Matt looked to the one wearing the bowler as he became increasingly uncomfortable in his own skin.

"I heard about him, Luke," Matt said. "If this is John Slocum . . ."

"If this is John Slocum, then we're about to become rich. Both of us. Now shut up and do like we planned."

"If you planned on dying," Slocum warned, "you're both going about it the right way."

JAKE LOGAN

SLOCUM AND THE WARM RECEPTION

JOVE BOOKS, NEW YORK

THE BERKLEY PUBLISHING GROUP
Published by the Penguin Group
Penguin Group (USA) Inc.
375 Hudson Street, New York, New York 10014, USA

USA I Canada I UK I Ireland I Australia I New Zealand I India I South Africa I China

Penguin Books Ltd., Registered Offices: 80 Strand, London WC2R 0RL, England
For more information about the Penguin Group, visit penguin.com.

SLOCUM AND THE WARM RECEPTION

A Jove Book / published by arrangement with the author

Jove Books are published by The Berkley Publishing Group.
JOVE® is a registered trademark of Penguin Group (USA) Inc.
The "J" design is a trademark of Penguin Group (USA) Inc.

For information, address: The Berkley Publishing Group,
a division of Penguin Group (USA) Inc.,
375 Hudson Street, New York, New York 10014.

ISBN: 978-0-515-15382-8

PUBLISHING HISTORY
Jove mass-market edition / August 2013

PRINTED IN THE UNITED STATES OF AMERICA

10 9 8 7 6 5 4 3 2 1

Cover illustration by Sergio Giovine.

This is a work of fiction. Names, characters, places, and incidents either are the product
of the author's imagination or are used fictitiously, and any resemblance to actual persons,
living or dead, business establishments, events, or locales is entirely coincidental.
The publisher does not have any control over and does not assume any responsibility for
author or third-party websites or their content.

ALWAYS LEARNING   PEARSON

1

The Smoke Creek Desert wasn't much more than a twenty-mile stretch of misery situated just over a day's ride north of Reno. John Slocum had left Reno with plenty of supplies, a full belly, and a fat pouch of gold and silver tucked deep into his saddlebag. Sure, most of that gold and silver was dust or chunks smaller than a child's fingernail, but it all added up just the same. Reno had been a good stop for Slocum in many respects. Even though he'd lost a bit at the card tables, the games were pleasant enough due to some fine company who always kept the whiskey flowing. The job that had brought him to Reno had led to a string of more work, all of which added up to the aforementioned pouch hidden at the bottom of his saddlebag.

Yes indeed, Slocum thought as he tapped his heels against the sides of his spirited gelding, coming to Reno had been the best choice he'd made in a while. His timing in leaving Reno, on the other hand, couldn't have been worse.

He was on a patch of trail with a whole lot of nothing on either side when he caught sight of two Indians on a high ridge to the west. Their silhouettes weren't very distinctive, but the way they sat atop their horses and kept pace with him without stirring so much as a bit of dust in their wake told him plenty. Slocum may not have noticed them at all if he hadn't gotten a peculiar feeling raking along the back of his neck like a set of ghostly fingertips. When he turned around, Slocum swatted at his neck in case an insect had landed there. Instead, that little itch was caused by whatever sense a man had that let him know when steely eyes had been watching him for a bit too long from the other side of a saloon or if a bobcat was skulking along the tree limb just above his head. Slocum didn't know what caused such a sense, but that itch had saved his life more times than he could count.

When he twisted around again, he could only find a single rider on the top of that ridge. A second later, that rider ducked low over his horse's neck and disappeared with a few quick snaps of his reins. "Damn," Slocum grunted under his breath as his hand went reflexively for the .44-caliber Smith & Wesson at his hip. Instead of drawing the pistol, he reached for the boot on his saddle to pat the Sharps rifle kept there. For the time being, it was enough to know the guns were there. He thought back to when he'd made preparations for his ride and recalled that he had, indeed, loaded the rifle. Although he didn't see the elusive rider, every instinct in his body told him that they had been Indians. Perhaps Slocum knew as much due to years of dealing with all sorts of men. One thing he'd gathered after dealing with gunmen of all shapes, sizes, and colors was that it took someone intimately familiar with their terrain to sneak up on John Slocum, and nobody was more familiar with their home soil than an Indian.

Slocum wasn't fearful when he flicked his reins to urge the gelding into a faster trot. Whether his instincts were right or not, he was only passing through those parts on his way to the next town. This wasn't his first time crossing the

Smoke Creek Desert. He'd spent a considerable amount of time in a town called Mescaline situated along its northern border and was crossing the dusty expanse now to trade his gold and silver to a fellow he knew there. He also knew there were a few settlements along the way, so Slocum set his sights to the north and hoped whoever was watching him would lose interest.

A few hours later, he spotted another silhouette.

This one sat tall and proud upon his horse's back, studying Slocum from on high as if he were watching an ant scurry from one mound of dirt to another. Not only did Slocum trust his instincts from before, but he added one more word to his assessment. Instead of Indian, it was now Indian brave. That was a very important distinction, and when a man saw a brave for the first time, there was no mistaking another one for as long as he lived. Of course, the trickiest part was to live for more than a minute or two after seeing what a brave was capable of doing.

Of one thing, Slocum was certain: Braves often hunted in packs. As he rode faster down the trail, he cast his eyes back and forth along the horizon. Every so often, he took a quick glance over one shoulder and then the other. Even when he pulled back on the reins and situated himself as if he was easy in the saddle, Slocum was still wary. The easygoing mannerism was to let anyone else know that he wasn't afraid. Like any other predator, men tended to become bolder when their prey showed weakness. Soon, he saw there was more than one predator watching him.

The first figure he picked out was easy enough to see, since it was still sitting bolt-straight and perched upon the highest ground in the vicinity. Slocum looked around for more, and while the other two weren't as easy to spot, he found them creeping up on him from both sides of the trail like a set of pincers tightening around unsuspecting meat.

"You men can stop right where you are!" Slocum

announced. "I know you're there and I'll shoot if you get any closer."

Both men approaching the trail did so like overgrown snakes. They crawled on their bellies within the scrub bushes, their legs stretched out behind them and wrapped in skins, which allowed them to blend in with the desert floor. The exposed skin of their bare backs was raw after being scratched and scraped by dry branches and exposed rocks. Even though he'd spotted them, Slocum was unable to tell where the would-be ambushers were looking. He assumed they glanced upward for a signal from their leader.

"These are not your lands, white man," the brave on horseback said from his lofty perch.

"Never claimed they were," Slocum replied. "I'm just passing through."

"So say all the other white men before they bring wagons of guns and fill our nights with fire."

"You've been watching me long enough to know that I've done nothing but ride since I left Reno. I got no wagon," Slocum said as he sat up straight and raised both hands high above his head. "I'm no soldier."

"You have guns," the brave said. "All white men carry guns."

Slocum slowly lowered his hands and turned his horse around to face the ridge where the brave was watching. He could feel tension ripple through the air like the forerunner of a thunderstorm as the snakes in the bushes on either side of the trial coiled in preparation to strike. "You gonna tell me you're not armed?" Slocum asked.

The brave had no response to that.

"Tell you what," Slocum said. "I'm headed north and don't intend on stopping unless I need to sleep or get a drink. This trail is worn well enough to mean I ain't the first man to travel it. Folks have been coming through here for a long time. Even I came through these parts some time ago and not one feather in any of the tribes was ruffled."

Like a cold, rasping wind blowing in from the top of an ice-capped mountain, the brave said, "That was before."

"Before what?"

"Before I claimed this road for my own. I warned your lawmen not to come here any longer and it seems they still need proof that I am not to be taken lightly."

"Who the hell are you?" Slocum asked.

That got a reaction from the brave. In fact, Slocum's question, spoken in such a flippant manner, caused the brave to glower down at him and shout, "I am the wrath of my people! I am the voice of these lands! Since an example needs to be made, I will use your blood to make it!"

That was all Slocum needed to hear. Plenty of men went on about their causes or whatever may have riled them up enough to take action, but it always boiled down to one thing: Was that man a killer? Slocum wasn't able to see the brave's eyes, which would have helped in that regard. He was a good judge of when a man was blowing smoke or not and this one was too angry to be making any sort of bluff. From that point on, he didn't care what example the brave wanted to set or what injustices had been done to him. All he wanted was to put the raving Indian behind him, and if that could be done without bloodshed, all the better.

In one quick string of motions, Slocum brought his horse around to its original course and snapped his reins. The gelding responded perfectly and launched into motion amid the clatter of hooves against sun-baked ground. The Indians on either side of the trail let out war cries as they leapt up from the scrub with knives in hand. One of them nicked Slocum's boot but didn't dig in deep enough to draw any blood. Another must have caught the horse because the gelding lurched to one side and whinnied in surprise.

Anger more than anything else caused Slocum to draw his .44 and twist around to the side opposite of where his boot had been nicked. Another Indian was there, plain as day, in Slocum's line of sight. His hair was cut close to the scalp on both sides of his head, leaving only a narrow strip plastered to his head like a filthy mane. The Indian's eyes glinted beneath several layers of mud caked onto his face to form a mask. When he saw the gun in Slocum's hand, the Indian showed no fear or hesitation before opening his mouth wide to howl crazily up at him.

2

Slocum pulled his trigger quickly because he wanted to keep the Indian from grabbing hold of his leg. While Slocum had seen too many things in his years to be afraid of much, there was no shame in being startled by an animal as wild as this one. The .44 barked once and sent a round sparking against the rocky surface of the trail.

Another war cry sounded from behind Slocum as the brave rode down from the rise. That shout was quickly followed by the crack of a rifle being fired and the hiss of a round whipping through the air within inches of Slocum's ear. Since that first shot was so close to hitting its mark, Slocum knew it wouldn't take long for the brave to put his target down. Suddenly, the prospect of getting away from those crazed Indians wasn't so appealing. It was time to stand and fight.

The Indian with the narrow mane of hair was still in his sight, so Slocum took an extra moment to aim before squeezing his trigger again. That bullet tore through the Indian's hip, but somehow failed to slow him down. Whatever had sparked the fire in that one's eyes was powerful enough to keep it burning as he charged forward without showing a lick of concern for pain or the threat of death. All the conviction in the world wouldn't have been enough to keep him on his feet when Slocum swung down from his saddle while lashing out with a boot to knock him in the face. The momentum of his entire body was behind his boot heel as he met the oncoming Indian with one hell of a nasty reception. The Indian's head snapped back, and blood spewed from a freshly opened cut in his face as his arms and legs flailed.

Slocum hit the ground with one foot, planted the other, and spun around to greet the next attacker. The other Indian that had crawled up to the trail didn't present himself right away. Another shot was fired from the brave behind him, causing Slocum to hunch down even lower. Although the gelding had backed away in the midst of all that ruckus, he wasn't about to leave Slocum by himself. Once he'd put several paces between himself and the fighting men, the horse held its ground.

After enough time had passed for the brave to lever another round into whatever rifle was in his hands, Slocum dove forward and stretched out one arm to cushion his impact while twisting his entire body around. The brave's shot came right on schedule and whipped through the air a foot or so above Slocum's body. If he'd still been upright at the time, he would have caught that round squarely in the chest.

Slocum's shoulder and back pounded against the ground. Even if he'd expected the wind to be knocked from his lungs, there wasn't a whole lot he could do to brace for it. Since he'd managed to keep enough breath inside to sustain him for another second or two, he gritted his teeth and sighted along the top of his .44. The Indian with the coarse mane on his head was coming at him again, eyes burning with crazy fire. Slocum pulled his trigger once, hit his mark, and fired again.

The first shot punched into the Indian's chest and the

second drilled a hole through a face that was already covered in a mess of blood put there by Slocum's boot heel. He fell backward and sprawled to the dusty ground, feet scraping at the desert as if he still thought he was taking a run at Slocum.

Rather than waste a shot in putting a quick end to the first Indian, Slocum looked for the second. That one wasn't hard to find, since he'd almost gotten close enough to put an even quicker end to Slocum using a short-handled tomahawk. The little axe was gripped in a tight fist held close to the Indian's ear. Slocum could just make out the man's face before his eyes were drawn to the tomahawk's sharpened stone edge as it was swung at him. Slocum leaned back to allow the tomahawk to slice past him so close that he could feel the gust of wind in its wake.

Unlike his companion, the second Indian wasn't crazy. When Slocum fired a quick shot at him, he hopped to one side in the hopes of avoiding incoming fire. The shot had been taken in haste, but provided Slocum with some breathing room so he could circle away from the tomahawk.

Rather than decorate himself with war paint of any kind, the second Indian had smeared mud across his entire face and chest. His head was shaved clean and covered with mud. Because of a similar coating on his arms and legs, he'd been close to invisible while crawling on the ground. That struck a chord in the back of Slocum's mind.

He'd seen other Indians use similar tactics, which had forced him to deal with one hell of a mess. Rather than take the time to think if these were the same Indians he'd dealt with before, Slocum busied himself with the act of staying alive.

That tomahawk was in very capable hands, cutting through the air in short, efficient chops. As soon as Slocum leaned away to avoid one swing, the weapon was brought up and back around to take another. He ducked under that attack and snuck a sharp jab into the other man's gut. The

Indian let out a wheezing grunt and staggered back a step, allowing Slocum to back away as well.

"One man's dead," Slocum said between gulping breaths. "No need to make it two."

"It will be two," the Indian replied in a voice that struck Slocum as peculiar. "When you are laid out for the vultures." With that, the Indian lunged again.

Slocum had been doing his best to keep track of the brave with the rifle. Unfortunately, that was tough to do when so much of his attention was focused on someone else. Knowing he was in danger by being on open ground, Slocum broke into a run that was in such a crooked line he must have appeared to be drunk. Appearances were the farthest thing from his mind, however, as he zigged one way and zagged another. The erratic strategy paid off when the brave's next shot tore through empty space.

Slocum was heading for his horse, and because the animal was content to let him get there, he was certain he could get to the Sharps rifle holstered in the saddle's boot. He was close enough to smell the sweat soaked into the gelding's coat when he heard the crunch of feet against the ground directly behind him. Slocum spun around to find the mud-caked Indian racing toward him with his tomahawk cocked back next to his ear. Slocum faced the Indian head-on while backing toward his horse. Once again proving to be more calculating than his deceased partner, the Indian slowed to a halt.

Both men circled each other for several long seconds.

The Indian watched Slocum carefully as Slocum did his best to watch both the man directly in front of him and the brave that was still on horseback. The brave was outside the .44's range but well within the reach of his rifle. He had the weapon's stock to his shoulder and glared at Slocum over the top of its long barrel. Slocum adjusted his steps to put the closest Indian between himself and the one with the rifle.

"Leave your horse and guns and you can walk away," the muddy Indian said.

Slocum narrowed his eyes. "What happened to all the big talk from before? Seeing a man get gunned down take some of the starch from your collar?"

"No," the Indian said with a slow shake of his head. "I've seen plenty of men die. Looks like I'm about to watch another."

Instead of waiting for the Indian to make the next move, Slocum took those words as a declaration of intent. He lunged for his horse and almost frightened the gelding away before his fingers scraped against the stock of the Sharps. As much as he hated to put his back to the Indian, Slocum had to turn around so he could reach across the horse's back and retrieve the rifle. Just as his body was stretched and his arm was extended toward the Sharps, the Indian lunged at him like a rattlesnake going in for the kill.

Slocum sidestepped to avoid getting sliced straight down the middle. When the stone blade dug into the saddle far enough to cause the gelding to rear up in pain, Slocum almost wished he had absorbed that blow. Fortunately, Slocum was now able to take the Sharps from the boot.

Just because he had the rifle didn't mean he was in the clear. In fact, Slocum couldn't put the Sharps to proper use because he still had the .44 in his right hand. He meant to holster the pistol so he could put a finger on the rifle's trigger, but the muddy Indian wasn't about to give him the chance. After plucking his tomahawk from where it had been lodged in the saddle's thick leather, he came at Slocum like a whirlwind.

From there, the fight became nothing short of chaos. Both men ripped into each other, ducked, sidestepped, and swung again in an all-out frenzy. Slocum survived the first onslaught by focusing only on the blade of the tomahawk as it came at him again and again. Every now and then, he snuck in a quick jab or a sharp knee driven into the Indian's side. Slocum could feel his knuckles and leg pounding against solid flesh, but wasn't able to slow the other man down. Suddenly, the Indian's filthy face filled his field of vision. Slocum could see the Indian's elbow and forearm as they came around in a vicious semicircle with the tomahawk trailing like the cutting end of a whip.

Slocum dropped straight down while letting out a quick profanity along with what was left of his breath. There was a sharp clang, after which the Indian stopped dead in his tracks. When he stood up again, Slocum saw the tomahawk had become lodged in the canteen that hung from his saddle horn by a strap.

The Indian winced with the effort of pulling the weapon's blade from the metal container. Although he was able to free the tomahawk, it wasn't before Slocum stood up and raised his gun. Opening his mouth to let out another war cry, the Indian cocked back the tomahawk in preparation of a strong downward chop. Before he could follow through, the Indian was rocked by the last round from Slocum's .44.

At point-blank range, the shot could only be heard as a muffled thump. The Indian was lifted off both feet and sent staggering backward with blood pouring from a hole in his chest as well as a much larger one in his back. By the time the Indian fell over, Slocum had tossed the .44 and was turning the sights of the Sharps rifle toward the brave on horseback. "You brought this on yourself," he shouted. "Still want to take it further?"

The brave stared silently back at him. Despite the distance between both men, they might as well have been inches away from each other. In fact, as he waited for a response, a word, even a flinch, Slocum swore he could see the man behind that other rifle blink.

"What tribe are you from?" Slocum asked.

The brave did not respond.

"Who are your people? Where is your homeland?" Even though there was nothing to make him think he was going to get an answer, Slocum kept asking his questions. "What did you expect to do out here like this? How many others have you killed?" That last question brought Slocum's blood to a boil. "That's it, isn't it? You've ambushed others on this trail. Lord knows plenty of folks use it to get across the state line into Oregon. Probably ranchers and families looking to move on up into California or maybe into Canada. They didn't put up as much of a fight as all this, is that it?"

Still, the brave held his tongue.

The longer the silence went on, the more Slocum had to fight to keep from pulling his trigger. Eventually, the brave lowered the rifle from his shoulder. Soon after that, his head drooped slightly forward and he steered his horse so it was facing another direction. Once he knew he'd made it that far without being shot, he started to ride away.

"Not so fast!" Slocum called out.

Surprisingly enough, the brave stopped.

Studying the other man through a stern scowl, Slocum said, "I'll have that rifle."

The brave stayed put.

"You don't have to bring it here," Slocum amended. "Just leave it in that spot right there."

Slowly, the brave extended his arm. In a motion that was surprisingly quick, he brought the rifle back up to his shoulder and took aim. Slocum already had his Sharps at the ready. He'd had plenty of time to take aim and all he needed to do was squeeze the trigger. The Sharps barked once, sent its round through the air, and dropped the brave like a bottle from a fence post.

Even after the brave fell, Slocum watched and waited for something else to happen. Perhaps more Indians would emerge from where they'd been hiding to pick him off with bullets, arrows, or blades. Perhaps another brave would circle around to try and get the jump on him. Truth be told, he didn't really know what to expect. The ambush seemed strange from the moment it started and it ended in much the same way.

Eventually, the sun beating down upon his head, neck, and shoulders made Slocum lower his Sharps so he could wipe away a trickle of sweat that stung one of his eyes. Every rustling wind he heard, every scrape of something against a rock or movement of a dry branch, made him think the attack would continue. Nothing he saw could back that up, however.

There was nothing to see apart from the two dead men lying sprawled upon the ground.

Slocum propped his rifle against a rock near the Indian caked in mud. Taking one knee to present a smaller target if there was anyone out there still interested in taking a shot at him, he emptied the Smith & Wesson's cylinder of spent casings and then fed it fresh rounds from his gun belt. The movements were as common to him as drawing breath, which meant he didn't need to look at what he was doing. His eyes were plenty busy as his fingers prepared the .44 for another fight, however. They darted back and forth, never stopping, never satisfied with all of the nothing they found.

Finally, when the pistol was full and its cylinder snapped shut, he got to his feet and stayed there. Slocum no longer thought about making it difficult for someone to take a shot at him. On the contrary, he stayed as still as the rest of the desert . . . daring any other would-be ambushers to do their worst. His features took on a hard edge, and when he spat upon the ground, he might as well have been spitting into the faces of every one of the cowardly sons of bitches that had tried to ambush him.

At least the first two had gone out fighting. Slocum looked down at them while holstering the .44, focusing his attention on the one covered in mud. He squatted down and turned the dead man's head so he could look at his face. Something about him just wasn't right. When his canteen had been chopped by the tomahawk, it had spilled its contents onto the ground not far away from where the body now rested. Slocum went over to dip his fingers into the water so he could brush the moisture against his parched lips. There was a little left in the lower portion of the canteen, perhaps enough for two or three gulps, but not enough to get him all the way to Mescaline. Instead of riding to the more familiar town, Slocum would need to stop over at one of the smaller settlements along the way. He only hoped the places he recalled hadn't dried up and blown away like everything else in the arid climate.

Running his hand through the spilled water was barely enough to get his fingers damp. The desert had soaked up the rest of the water already, leaving just enough for him to clear away some of the dirt caked onto the dead Indian's face. That little bit of progress was enough to put a thoughtful scowl onto his face.

"Well now," he muttered. "If you were such a mad dog killer, I'm guessing someone might be looking for you. And if that's the case," he said while positioning himself at the Indian's head so he could slip both hands under the corpse's shoulders, "then someone might pay a dollar or two to the man that found you."

The Indian may not have been a big fellow, but he was now deadweight. It wasn't easy bringing him to the spot where Slocum's horse was waiting, and when he got there, Slocum was ready to be done with the entire task. The raiding party had to have horses somewhere. Even if they were tough and crazy, those Indians still needed something other than bare feet to cover miles of scorched earth. But the longer Slocum stayed in that spot, the more he wanted to leave it. There were things to be done and less time in which to do them so he eased the body off his shoulder to drape it across the back of his horse. The gelding shifted and fussed beneath the weight, but quickly settled down.

"Don't worry, boy," Slocum said as he climbed into the saddle. "You won't have to drag this extra weight for long."

3

By Slocum's recollection, there were a few towns scattered in or around the desert to the south of Mescaline, but he wouldn't have been at all surprised to find skeletal remains of a settlement instead. When he saw a hint of smoke rising like a smear being slowly dragged to the west, Slocum felt the touch of hope. If that smoke came from the stack of a steam engine, it could mean at least one of those settlements he'd glimpsed some time ago had fallen upon a bit of good fortune.

Slocum's good fortune came when he saw a thriving little cluster of well-maintained buildings in a spot where he'd been expecting a ghost town. He pointed his gelding's nose in that direction and rode as quickly as he could until he reached a sign that let him know he'd crossed into the town limits of a place called Davis Junction.

Apparently, some time during the years since he'd last made his way through the Smoke Creek Desert, a railroad line had been laid down and this town had reaped its reward. As the trail became a proper street and more businesses showed up on either side, Slocum glanced back at the load he was carrying. The dead Indian hadn't gone anywhere. In fact, since the sun was hot enough to bake the muddy flesh into a texture similar to rough pottery or cracked clay, the sight wasn't as bad as when they'd started riding together. Even so, it was still a sight that drew some attention.

Plenty of folks took notice of him and his grisly cargo as he made his way farther into town. Having caught sight of the sheriff's office right away, he steered for the squat little building down the street from the long train station that looked to be the center of Davis Junction. Even before he reined his horse to a stop in front of the office, a gnarled old-timer in a wide-brimmed hat and sweat-soaked shirt walked to the edge of the little porch outside the sheriff's front door.

"Hello there," the old-timer said while hooking both thumbs over his belt. "Looks like you've had a hell of a mornin'."

Slocum looked down at him and replied, "Would you believe I feel worse than I look?"

"Sure would, especially seein' as how you rode in on something other than a train. Desert or no, it still seems you're doing a whole lot better than that one right there."

Since the old man was pointing to the gelding's back, Slocum looked over there as if he didn't know what had caught his eye. "Yeah. Thought I'd let the law know about my guest before too many eyebrows were raised. So, are you the man I need to talk to?"

For a moment, the old-timer looked stunned. He even shifted to glance over his shoulder as if Slocum had suddenly gained the ability to look straight through him. Finally, he said, "Me? I'm just a deputy."

"What's your name?"

"Patrick."

"John Slocum," he said while extending a hand.

The deputy shook Slocum's hand with vigor. "Pleased to meet ya! I heard tell about what happened in Mescaline the last time you were there. So . . . you some kind of bounty hunter?"

Slocum didn't appreciate being lumped in with the kind of scum that generally found work collecting bounties. Reminding himself that he'd ridden into town with a corpse strapped to the back of his horse put things back into perspective. "I'm not a bounty hunter," he told the deputy. "I just crossed paths with this one and a couple of his friends about ten miles outside of town."

Another set of boots knocked against the boards in front of the sheriff's office. The man in them wore battered jeans and a brown shirt beneath what had probably once been a fairly elegant suit jacket. Although the garment may have started off as a fine specimen, whatever dandy it had been tailored for was most definitely not the man who wore it now. He was a few inches taller than Patrick and at least ten years the deputy's junior. Coal black stubble marred a lean face accented by a thin nose that cut a straight line between a pair of high cheekbones. While he didn't draw a gun, he placed his hands upon his hips as if to display the holster wrapped around his waist.

"How many friends were there?" the younger man asked. His jacket may have been a bit too big for him and the buttons had lost their shine, but the star pinned to his chest sure hadn't.

"You'd be the sheriff?" Slocum asked.

The younger man nodded. "Marshal."

"Sorry. You're the marshal."

"No. I'm Sheriff Marshal."

"Which is it?"

As the younger man let out a tired sigh, Patrick chuckled nervously. "Marshal is his family name," he explained. "Funny bit of luck him becoming sheriff."

"Could be worse," Slocum said with a grin,

With patience that was clearly strained, the lawman said, "I know. I could have been *Marshal* Marshal."

"Heard that one already?" Slocum asked.

"Many times. Tell me what happened to put you in the possession of that poor soul laying across your horse's rump. Not that that isn't a perfect spot for him."

"Sounds to me like you two are already acquainted."

"Could be. Depends on your story."

"You mind if I put my horse up first?" Slocum asked. "He's got a few cuts that need tending and after that I could use something to drink."

"You came into my town with a dead body, mister. I'd say that means you owe me an explanation."

"All right then. The first part of my explanation is that I've been in the desert for a few days. Isn't that enough of a reason for me to want to take care of my horse as well as my own thirst?"

The lawman may have been younger than his deputy, but the longer Slocum looked at him, the more years he tacked on to his estimate of the sheriff's age. By the time Marshal let out his next breath, he seemed to be even older. Slocum took that as a good sign. Usually honest lawmen were a lot wearier than crooked ones.

"Patrick," Marshal said, "how about you show this man to a place where he can see to his horse and get some water?"

"Right away, Sheriff."

Leveling a stern glare at Slocum, the sheriff added, "Because of the circumstances of your arrival, I'll have to ask that your guns and that body stay here with me. You can collect them after I sort through what brings you to Davis Junction."

"All I'll want is my guns back," Slocum said as he handed them over. "You can keep the body."

"Strangers bearing gifts," Marshal sighed. "A fine way to end the day."

Patrick wasn't much of a guide, which suited Slocum just fine since he wasn't in the mood for a proper tour. Even if the deputy was intent on showing him the sights, Davis Junction didn't have many to offer. After seeing as many little towns as Slocum had throughout his years of riding from one to another, they all started looking alike. It wasn't until he'd spent some time walking a town's streets and swapping stories with the folks who lived there that he got a real sense of a place. Until then, every town was just a collection of buildings divided by a street or two.

There was a general store and a couple smaller places that offered dry goods.

There was a tailor and a blacksmith.

There were places to buy a meal.

Of course there were saloons.

Scattered here and there were houses as well as other places of business that Slocum didn't bother studying. Perhaps he saw a dentist's office situated up on a second floor. One thing that caught his eye was the small group of men clustered around a little telescope set up on a tripod. There was another cluster farther on, both sets of men being within spitting distance of the railroad tracks running through town.

As soon as Slocum spotted the livery stable close to the end of the street that Patrick had chosen, he didn't care about much of anything else. The gelding had done well to make it this far and was young enough to keep going without a fuss despite the cuts and scratches he'd collected during the fight. Even so, Slocum wanted to get him into a clean stall where the saddle could be unbuckled from his back. Patrick made small talk with a liveryman as Slocum saw to it that those things were done. Once the gelding had his snout cooling in a trough of water, Slocum patted his side and draped the saddlebags over one shoulder.

"How much for the stall?" Slocum asked.

The liveryman was a tall weed of a man with filthy gloves covering his hands and an old smock stained with whatever he'd fallen into while cleaning out his barn. "How long will you be needing it?"

"Don't know yet. Probably just a day or two."

"My price normally includes a grooming for the horse. Usually a nice brushing and such. You probably saw the sign posted out front."

"Yeah," Slocum said, although he didn't know what the hell the liveryman was referring to.

"I do that to stay competitive with the stable down the street, but if you wouldn't mind forsaking the brushing, I'll take a piece off the price." Wiping his hands on the spot of his smock that was the least stained with manure, he added, "I've had my fill of cleaning for one day."

"I'd be willing to pay a bit more than the daily rate if you tend to those cuts on my horse's sides. How's that grab ya?" Slocum asked.

"I can do that . . . for an extra dollar."

"Per day?"

"Just a one-time fee," the liveryman said with a shrug.

"Deal."

Both men shook hands and Slocum settled up for the first day's rate using some coins kept in a pouch strung around his neck. On his way out, he caught sight of a pretty little filly in the stall closest to the door. She was the kind of filly who walked on two legs, had long blond hair that was straight as straw, and wore a white cotton dress that clung to her body thanks to the sweat she'd worked up while fixing a latch on the stall's door.

"How'd I miss you?" Slocum asked as he walked by.

She smiled and turned her head. When she looked back at him, the blond woman showed Slocum a pair of eyes that were the same blue as the sky on the first day of spring. "Keep walking, mister," she said. "Plenty of work to be done."

Slocum meant to have a few more words with her, but was convinced to keep moving by a sharp knock on his back from a bony hand. "You heard the lady, John," Patrick said. "Keep walking."

"Am I under arrest?"

"No, but she ain't the only one that's got a job to do."

"Am I still allowed to have some water?" Slocum asked.

The deputy tipped his hat to the blonde and gave Slocum another shove. "Sure you are. There's a place on the way back to the sheriff's office that serves up some mighty fine pie along with that water. I think I'll join you."

Now that he was outside of the stable and the door had been kicked shut, Slocum put his back to the place and started walking. "She a friend of yours?"

"No. She's a distraction. You still got some explaining to do to the sheriff and he won't tolerate distractions."

"We have time. I'm not even armed, remember?"

Patrick nodded halfheartedly.

"Who is that lady?" Slocum asked. When an answer wasn't forthcoming, he added, "She your sister?"

"Not hardly," the deputy chuckled. "She does tend to turn heads."

"I suppose we have that in common."

"That you do, friend. That you do." Patrick stopped and took a quick peek back at the stable before lowering his voice and saying, "You don't seem like the sort who's looking to plant any roots in a town like this."

"What's that got to do with anything?"

"It means you'll be moving on sooner rather than later. That also means it's in your best interest to steer clear of trouble so as to make your stay here a pleasant one."

Slocum grinned. "Sounds like you've given that little speech once or twice before."

"I give it plenty of times," Patrick told him. "To damn near every vagrant or wayward miner that wanders in from the desert. It's good advice."

"For a vagrant or a miner perhaps. I ain't neither."

"You seem like a good enough fella, John. Mind if I call you that?"

"It's the name I was given."

Pointing back toward the stable, Patrick said, "That lady

back there is mighty pretty and you ain't the first to take notice. Plenty of fights been started on her account."

"Is she married?"

"No. Just real pretty and she knows it. Sometimes that's a lot worse than just being married."

"What kind of trouble has been started?" Slocum asked.

"Fights and such. One man wants to take a run at her and another gets the same idea in his head. Next thing you know, they're locking horns like a couple of rams in a field."

"Doesn't that sort of thing happen a lot when women are involved? At least, often enough that it's not a very new predicament."

"It ain't a new predicament," Patrick snapped. "And this ain't my first time wearing a tin star. I ain't no fool. I've kept the peace in plenty of towns bigger than this one, and a big part of doing that is knowing where the trouble lays. That little thing back there is trouble. It don't just follow her. She stirs it up and she enjoys every bit of it."

Slocum nodded. "I've met a few women like that."

"There's something else about her, though. I think she used to be a whore in California. Some say she cheated some poor soul out of every dime he earned sifting through river dirt in the Rockies."

"Doesn't explain why she's cleaning horse manure."

"Could be she's laying low," Patrick explained as he started walking again. Since Slocum was following him, he slipped back into his former easygoing mannerisms. "Could be she's waiting for some kind of storm to pass. Perhaps she's biding time before she can get to that money she stole. Who knows? All I do know is that she's got a wicked glint in her eye that I don't like."

"I've met other women with that glint," Slocum said with a wink. "Wicked women know plenty of things that sweet ones don't."

Patrick leaned over so he could whisper as they passed a long porch in front of a clothing store, where a few elderly women in dreary dresses with high collars watched them. "I ain't just talking about curling yer toes . . ."

Despite the deputy's best efforts to keep his voice down, one of the old ladies must have had ears sharper than an eagle's eye because she recoiled and grimaced as if Patrick had taken the Lord's name in vain. After she'd taken the time to lean over and whisper to the old woman beside her, both of them glared at Slocum and Patrick as if they were trying to burn holes through their heads.

"Ladies," Patrick said in a futile attempt to win them over. Even his crooked grin and hat tip weren't enough to remove some of the venom from the women's eyes. "Come on in here," he said while leading the way into a general store beneath a sign advertising ointments and other assorted medicinal offerings. There was a large counter along the side wall with a skinny bald man behind it and a row of stools in front of it.

Following the deputy's lead, Slocum took a seat. "This where I can have some of that pie you mentioned or did you just duck in here to escape the notice of them crones?"

"Ain't escaping from no one," Patrick grumbled. Having caught the skinny man's eye, he asked, "What's Martha cooked up today?"

The man behind the counter looked at Slocum nervously before replying, "Peach and rhubarb."

"I'll have a slice of the peach!"

"Fair warning, Pat. Them peaches are canned."

"We live in a desert," Patrick sneered. "You really think you needed to warn me about us not havin' peach trees?"

The skinny fellow shrugged and shifted his attention to Slocum. "What can I get for you, mister?"

"You can get me the name of someone who might know a thing or two about mining claims." Although he didn't have a claim in mind or any inquiry regarding one, any man who knew about claims would know someone who bought gold and silver. Seeing as how he was carrying a pouch of

the stuff in his saddlebags, Slocum wasn't exactly comfortable with making that fact known to anyone within earshot.
After all that had happened so far on his way to Mescaline,
the prospect of selling his dust and nuggets now and heading in another direction was becoming more and more
appealing.

The man behind the counter looked puzzled, but didn't
get a chance to speak before Patrick asked, "You planning
on staying around here for a spell?"

"That depends on what your sheriff has to say about it."

"I can't speak for him, but . . ." Looking at the skinny
fellow, the deputy snapped, "Go on and fetch that pie! Bring
us over a pitcher of water while you're at it."

The man behind the counter grumbled to himself and
shuffled away to fill the order.

Now, when Patrick lowered his voice, there wasn't anyone other than Slocum to hear him. A few locals were looking through a pile of blankets on the other side of the room
and the young man sitting at the farthest end of the counter
was too interested in his own business to bother eavesdrop-
ping on someone else's.

"That pretty lady cleaning them stalls is trouble," Patrick
said. "It's my business to handle trouble in this town and
I've found the best way to do that is to nip it in the bud before
it can sprout. Stay away from her, you hear?"

"Or what?" The question had come more as a knee-jerk
response and was out before Slocum could stop it. After so
many years of tending to his own affairs, good or bad, he
didn't care to take orders from others. He cared even less
for orders nestled within any kind of threat. Even so, he
immediately regretted being so cross with the deputy.

Patrick's face shifted into a harder expression. "Or . . . if
you go sniffing around her and any trouble follows, I can't
just assume she's the cause of it. You seem like a good fella,
John. I'm just warnin' you is all. The only reason I've been
pressing the matter so much is because I still got the eyes

and every other functioning part of a man and I know the first warning probably fell on deaf ears. Depending on how long you've been alone in that desert, the blood may have been rushing so fast that every warnin' I gave until this very second may not have been heard. So here it is again, watch that lady close."

Slocum nodded. "All right. I get the message. What did this woman do that's worth all these warnings?"

"Nothing I can prove," Patrick replied. "I heard some things, though. None of them were good."

"That's not exactly enough to hang your hat on."

"When she first came to town, some folks came looking for her in regard to a bit of violence in Montana. Seems the man she was with turned up dead. Another man who shared her company was an unsavory type and he wound up dead, too. Vigilantes strung him up and set him on fire."

"That seems awfully harsh," Slocum said. "Even for vigilantes."

"Rumor has it they did the lynching and she lit the match."

Slocum let out a low whistle. "These are just rumors?"

"Yep. There were also rumors that both men had it coming. The second fella was a known killer and the first wasn't known at all. Because of that, me and the sheriff kept her safe when those men came looking for her. They were armed and looking for blood and she . . . well . . . it just didn't seem proper to hand her over to men such as them."

"Understandable."

"Then the next batch came looking," Patrick continued. "That was just under a year ago. Bunch of wild-eyed owl hoots stinking of whiskey and shooting up the place like a pack of savages. In between all the cussing and yelling, they were asking for her, too. It was the law's duty to run them out of town no matter what they went on about, but they wanted to see her on account of her setting up a few of their friends to take a fall for something or other. Also said she stole a bundle of money from them."

"She didn't strike me as the rich sort," Slocum said.

"Not now, but she had enough to feed herself and buy a little house when she first arrived. She only started doing odd work here and there over the last few months after falling out of favor with some charitable sorts who took her under their wing after all them rough types came storming in looking to harm her."

"So she fell out of favor with them, huh?"

"Sure enough."

"Why?"

Patrick shrugged and leaned back as the man behind the counter approached with the pitcher of water and two cups. "Can't say for certain," the deputy replied. "I just know that, proof or not, there seems to be something to what I've been telling you other than just rumor."

After the man behind the counter went away to cut into the pie that was kept beneath an overturned pot on a table in one corner, Slocum poured himself some water and downed the entire cup in one gulp. The water was soaked into his body quicker than a drip disappeared from the surface of a frying pan. He poured himself another cup and allowed everything he'd heard to soak in along with the water. "I don't even know her name," he mused.

"You don't need to know much else than what I told you. I already repeated myself more than I like, so I ain't about to say anything else on the matter."

"Fair enough, I suppose. Think you can answer one question for me, though?"

"Depends on the question."

"If you have such strong suspicions about that woman, why did you bring me directly to that stable to put my horse up?"

Patrick hung his head as if he'd been expecting that question all this time and had just started to think he might not hear it. After a sigh, he told him, "Last time I checked, she was working at the stable just across the street from the sheriff's office. I arranged for her to work there so the sheriff and I could keep watch over her."

"I didn't see a stable near the sheriff's office."

"That's on account of me taking you in the other direction as quick as I could."

"Thanks for the warning, Pat. I'll keep it in mind. Since I don't intend on staying around town for long, I think I'll be just fine."

"You mentioned a day or two?"

"How about I leave tomorrow? Would that suit you?"

"I didn't mean to run you off," Patrick said. "Just givin' some friendly advice."

"I've got some business to take care of and I'd like to finish it quick."

"Business about them claims?" the man behind the counter asked as he shuffled forward with a hearty portion of peach pie on a chipped plate.

"You know someone who might be able to help in that regard?" Slocum asked.

"Reid Flanders is the man to talk to if you want to look up the legal right to a claim or buy one outright. He brokers sales for patches of land as well, since there ain't much mining going on in these parts. Not since the silver and copper was cleaned out a few years back."

"Sounds like just the man I need to speak to."

"His office is on the corner of Laramie and First. Head out of here and turn right. Can't miss it."

"Much obliged."

"Don't make any appointments yet, though," Patrick advised. "You got one with Sheriff Marshal if you forgot."

"I didn't forget, but it can wait."

Patrick's brow furrowed as he asked, "Wait for what?"

"Wait for me to have my pie." Looking to the skinny fellow, Slocum added, "Make mine rhubarb."

4

"What in the hell took you so long?" the sheriff bellowed as Slocum and Patrick entered his little office.

It had been less than an hour since they'd left the lawman's sight, but it seemed Marshal had been building up steam for a good deal longer than that.

"I went with him just like you said," Patrick told the lawman. "Had to put his horse up and whet his whistle. Ain't exactly proper to let a man go thirsty after he crawled in from the desert."

"Plenty of things crawl in from the desert," Marshal said. "Don't mean we have to treat them proper."

"Speaking of which," Slocum said as he walked into the sheriff's office and had a look around. "Where's the man I brought along with me?"

The office was a small building that was only slightly larger than a cabin. There was such a sparse amount of furnishings within that there was still room for three men to walk around. Patrick went to a gun cabinet and posted himself in front of it. The sheriff had come from around a desk that had more dust on top of it than paperwork. A small stack of newspapers was in one corner beside the door and the wall adjacent to that was covered in reward notices. Slocum had thought they were reward notices at first, but most turned out to be clippings from newspapers tacked up like a wide frame around three notices bearing the likenesses of half a dozen men.

Stepping up to Slocum's side, Marshal looked at the wall display as well. "Any of this look familiar?"

"Yep," Slocum replied. Extending one arm, he used a finger to jab at two of the likenesses that had been drawn in rough charcoal lines. "That man there and the one right beside him. They look similar to the ones who ambushed me in the desert. Can't speak for the third one. He kept his distance. If you want to see him, you can ride out and examine the corpse yourself."

As far as drawings went, the ones on the reward notices were crude. They did, however, depict the strange hair style of the Indian that had been coated in mud. The other one's face was comprised of simple lines which Slocum might have overlooked if he hadn't spent so much time with the man attached to it slung across the back of his horse.

"How many did you say there were?" Marshal asked.

Without hesitation, Slocum replied, "Three."

"And what did they do exactly?"

"One of them shouted down at me from a ridge while the other two crept up on either side so they could jump me from the bushes."

Rubbing his chin, the sheriff asked, "All three of them Indians?"

"That's what I thought at first," Slocum told him. "But I'm not so sure about the man I brought in."

"What about now?" Marshal said as he turned toward the office's back door and strode over to open it. "Take a look and tell me what you think now that I cleaned him up a bit."

Slocum followed the lawman outside to where the

Indian's body was propped against the back of the building with his feet stretched out in front of him as if he were merely sleeping off a bottle of hard liquor. The cleaning the sheriff had referred to had obviously been a few bucketfuls of water tossed onto the dead man's face. Enough of the caked mud had been cleared away to reveal features that didn't remind Slocum of any Indian he'd ever seen.

"Just like I figured," Slocum said. "He's no Indian."

"You got that right," Marshal said. "None of those men are. They're just a small band of robbers looking to put a scare into folks by making them think they've been set upon by an Injun war party. They know the desert like the backs of their hands and their ruse has been working well enough for them to stick with it and keep picking apart anyone that rides through."

Slocum thought back to the attack. "It didn't seem like a real raiding party, that's for certain, but the man leading it struck me as a brave."

"His name is Ellis Jaynes. Used to be a scout for the Cavalry, but was drummed out of his regiment for thievery. Knows just enough to put on a good show, but he usually keeps his distance and takes potshots with a rifle while his other men crawl in close for the dirty work. Usually stands up on high ground blathering on about him being the blood of his land or the wrath of his tribe or some other such nonsense. What's so damned funny?"

Slocum couldn't help but chuckle when he heard the sheriff's watered-down description. "Just seems to me like you've got a better handle on this whole thing than I thought."

"Glad to hear it. I suppose you knew about Jaynes when you rode into town?"

"Why would you think that?"

"Because you're John Slocum," the sheriff replied. "I've heard a thing or two about you."

"Whatever you heard, it doesn't mean I make it

my business to keep up on news about every little bunch of robbers that dress up like Indians to frighten folks on a desert road. The only reason I brought in one of them was because I suspected this wasn't the first time they've tried something like this."

"Then you're after a reward."

"It entered my mind there may be a price on their heads, but I thought the law might also want to know those men were dead. Since I did go through so much trouble, however, I'll take whatever reward is coming."

"I suppose you're entitled. Come back inside and I'll settle up with you."

Slocum and the sheriff went back inside. Marshal circled around his desk, opened a drawer, and removed a small metal box. He opened the box, took out a wad of cash, and peeled off two fifty-dollar bills. "Here you go," he said while handing over the money. "Paid in full."

Holding the money in his open hand, Slocum asked, "That's all for a known killer? A hundred dollars?"

The sheriff shrugged while closing the box and putting it back into his drawer. "Would have been more for Ellis Jaynes, but not much. Check the notice yourself if you think I'm lying."

Slocum looked over at the notice once again and focused on the figure written beneath the crudely drawn picture. "It says a hundred fifty," he pointed out.

"Fifty dollars makes that much difference to a man like you?" Marshal asked.

"I've got to pay for my meals the same as anyone. I also don't much care for being shortchanged on any job I do."

Without so much as glancing at the notices, Marshal said, "Check it again. The notice says a hundred and fifty . . . if he's brought in alive. There's a penalty for dead. If you would have thought to bring in all the bodies, there would have been more coming to you."

Slocum had to lean in closer to the notice, but he quickly

saw that the sheriff was correct. He closed his fist around the money he'd been given so he could stuff it into his pocket. "Guess that about wraps up our business, then. How about handing over my weapons?"

"I still have some questions for you, mister. Namely, why'd you only bring in one of them?"

"Because," Slocum replied, "there was a long ride ahead of me and I wasn't about to slow my horse down even more by hauling all that extra weight. I can tell you where to find the other ones if you're interested."

The sheriff dismissed that offer with half a wave of his hand. "I don't give a damn where the other bodies are. Feeding the coyotes would be the best thing them men have ever done. I'd like your word that you'd tell me if you knew where to find anyone else Jaynes may have associated with before they find some other gunhands willing to make some quick money by dressing as Indians and terrorizing another group of travelers on their way to my town."

"Why would I know such a thing?"

"I already told you," Marshal said. "I heard plenty about John Slocum and a lot of it involves you gunning down some killer or tracking down another. Seems about right that you'd know where to find Ellis Jaynes. You crossing paths with him and his raiders seems like too big of a coincidence for me to swallow."

"Then swallow a little harder, Sheriff," Slocum said. "Because a coincidence is all it was. Trust me, I've seen more than enough of them to spot another when I stumble through it."

The lawman eyed him carefully while slowly digesting everything he said. "You weren't here to look for Jaynes?"

"No, sir."

"Then what brings you to town?"

"I've got business in Mescaline," Slocum replied. "If you have any questions regarding my character, I propose you ask someone who's lived there for more than a year. They'll tell you my word is good enough to hold water. If I can conduct my business here, I'm willing to do so and be on my way."

Nodding slowly to himself, the sheriff shifted his focus back to his desk. Although there wasn't much there to catch anyone's eye, he busied himself with a few scraps of paper as he grumbled, "Yeah, I heard about what you did in Mescaline."

"Then you know I'm not just some vagrant. And you should also know there's no good reason to treat me like a criminal."

"If I was treating you that way, you'd be locked in the cage out back."

Slocum had seen the little shed behind the office when he'd poked his nose outside to get a look at the partially washed body. It wasn't the worst jail he'd seen cobbled together by a lawman without any other options, but it wasn't something he wanted to see up close. "Just give me my guns and I'll be going. Otherwise," Slocum added gravely, "I'd like to know what cause you have for keeping them from me."

The sheriff looked up at him intently. For a moment, it seemed the lawman was going to make a case for keeping the guns in his possession. Eventually, Marshal let out the breath he'd been hanging on to and looked at his deputy. "Go ahead and give Mr. Slocum his guns."

Patrick fished a key from his pocket, fit it into the cabinet behind him, and opened it to reveal a row of pistols hanging from pegs and a few rifles propped up beside a pair of shotguns. Slocum's Sharps was in there as well as the .44. After handing over the two weapons to Slocum, Patrick locked up the cabinet as if it contained a treasure of gold bricks.

"If it's all the same to you," Slocum said as he holstered the .44, "I'll find a suitable hotel on my own."

"There's three to choose from," Marshal said. "Have a good night's sleep." With that, the lawman looked down at his desk and scribbled on a single sheet of paper.

There was plenty Slocum wanted to say at that moment. Instead, he bit his tongue and left the sheriff to whatever nonsense had suddenly occupied him. The saddlebags had been slung over his shoulder throughout most of his time in Davis Junction, but they seemed especially cumbersome when he hefted them again now along with the Sharps as he went through the office door. Once outside, he broke into a stride that carried him across the street. Out of curiosity, he glanced over one shoulder to find the little stable that Patrick had mentioned earlier. "Nothing's ever easy," he snarled.

"Where are you going?" Patrick asked as he came from the office.

"What do you care? If that sheriff told you to keep an eye on me while I'm in town, he should do it himself."

"That ain't it." Huffing to catch up with Slocum, Patrick finally came alongside him and struggled to match his pace. "Don't take any of that personal. The sheriff hasn't lived around here as long as I have. He's still got dirt from Virginia on the bottom of his boots."

"What's that got to do with anything?"

"I'm saying all he knows about you is what he gathered from what he heard from others. He's been to Mescaline, but not when Jeremiah Hartley was runnin' the place. He never got to see the faces that was busted up or the fingers that were hacked off when folks couldn't afford to pay the taxes he levied."

Slocum stopped in his tracks. It wasn't often that he thought about Jeremiah Hartley, and part of that was because he tried not to dwell very long on the faces belonging to the men he'd killed. Whether those men had it coming or not was just a footnote that didn't make a scrap of difference on those nights when the ghosts came knocking. Snuffing out someone's life stained a man's soul. The act alone was a weight to bear, and guilt or innocence didn't make it any lighter. It should have, but it didn't. For a man like Slocum, who'd taken more than a dozen men's shares of lives, it was a weight that would have been damn near unbearable if he dwelled on it for long.

Also, there was always a chance that the preachers were right and the dead truly did take some sort of comfort in being remembered. The way Slocum saw it, Jeremiah Hartley was a cruel son of a bitch who didn't deserve the slightest bit of comfort as he rotted in the hole where he'd been buried.

After letting out a slow, tired breath, Patrick said, "Eh, you must have ridden from one end of this country to the other a few times over since the last time you suffered through this stretch of desert. You probably forgot all about Jeremiah Hartley."

"No," Slocum said. "I haven't forgotten."

"My point is, if the sheriff don't pay you the proper respect, it's out of ignorance and nothing more. All he's seen is what Mescaline is now."

"Am I free to go about my business?" Slocum asked.

"Naturally," Patrick said.

"Then that's what I aim to do. When I'm finished, I'll be on my way." Slocum tapped the edge of a finger against the brim of his hat and turned his back on the deputy. He could find Laramie Street on his own.

5

Reid Flanders was a typical blowhard. His belly was fat from too much town cooking and his hair was pasted to his scalp by sweat and a cheap concoction that smelled of musk and saddle leather. He wore his secondhand suit as if it did something to hide the guns strapped under his arm and to his hip. In the mood Slocum was in when he stepped inside the assayer's office, he wished the fat man would be stupid enough to make a move for one of those smoke wagons.

Just as Slocum had figured, any broker interested in mining claims was also interested in buying the ore that was dug out of them. After the tedious process of weighing some of the silver Slocum gave to him, Flanders winced and said, "Silver prices are down lately."

"Why's that?"

"Had a run on the stuff recently and I ain't been able to unload it. Broker I see every now and then from California ain't offering me as much as usual."

"That's not my problem," Slocum said.

"It's both our problems, mister. I can't get rid of it, then I can't pay as much for it. Now gold, on the other hand . . ."

Still carrying the saddlebag over one shoulder, Slocum shifted his feet as if he was suddenly more aware of the weight of the gold he'd left in his pouch. Coming to Reid's place now was a way to test the waters and see how much he could get from the broker. So far, he wasn't liking him well enough to trust him with the rest of what he'd brought.

"What's the best you can do on the silver?" Slocum asked.

"For what you got here . . . fifty dollars."

Truth be told, it was more than Slocum was expecting. He didn't let that show on his face when he asked, "Can you do sixty?"

The broker shook his head. "Only reason I'm giving you that much is to let you know I run a square business." Apparently, Reid knew when he was being sized up. A man in his line of work was under close scrutiny by anyone who walked through his door. "I can do fifty-five, but that's only if you agree to give me first crack at whatever you get a hold of next."

"What makes you think I have any more?"

"A man like yourself . . . riding into town with a dead outlaw strapped to your horse . . . trading unkind words with the sheriff . . . I'm guessing you'll acquire something else soon enough that you'd be wanting to trade for cash. Just so you know, I deal in all sorts of things other than gold and silver. Anything you might find valuable, just bring it my way. No questions asked."

"No questions, huh?"

Reid grinned and nodded. "That's right. I don't care where it come from—as long as I can sell it further down the line, I'm interested. Even the occasional stray animal. Know what I mean?"

Slocum nodded back at him, but only so he could get close enough to reach out and grab the broker by the front of his shirt. "I *do* know what you mean and I don't appreciate it!"

"I . . . I only . . . only meant that . . ."

"I know what you meant. You think I'm a horse thief or some damned ghoul who steals from dead folks and sells what I find to rodents like you."

"Not at all!" Reid protested. "Just a mistake! That's all it was, sir. I swear to you."

"You're damn right it was a mistake. Come to think of it, I imagine the bigger mistake was on the sheriff's part when he didn't look in your direction for word on where to find the real thieves around here."

Despite being lifted to his toes by Slocum's grip, the broker appeared offended as he quickly came to his own defense. "I've never stolen a thing in my life!"

"Maybe not, but you're willing to take stolen property and sell it. That tells me you have experience in this regard and I'm betting you must have built up a base of customers who do steal for a living. From what I've heard, a man named Ellis Jaynes could be one of your biggest clients."

Reid continued to shake his head. "All I do is broker transactions. Times being what they are and with us stuck out here in such rough terrain, folks have to do what they can to survive. They need to sell all sorts of things and I'm the one they come to. That's all."

"What about that talk concerning the stray animals?"

"Just what I said," Reid replied. "Recently I took some pigs off a man's hands for a good price. He told me he found them in an abandoned spread and I believed him. We both made a good profit."

Slocum didn't want to hear any more of what came out of the broker's mouth. It had been a trying day and the saddlebags were becoming particularly heavy on his shoulder, so he let Reid go and snarled, "I'll take that fifty dollars."

"Of course," he said. "Of course! My apologies for the misunderstanding, but I assure you that's all it was."

"Fine."

"Usually a man who hauls in the body of a wanted man

is always looking to make good money. He also tends to have various items land in his possession that he wants to sell. All I meant before was—"

"You want a good piece of advice?" Slocum offered.

"Certainly."

"Stop talking."

The broker swallowed hard, dug into his till, and took out the money he'd promised.

The room Slocum rented was above a saloon on Second Street. He didn't catch the name of the saloon, but was drawn there by the lack of noise that usually filled such a place. There was nobody playing a piano or banjo. No stage where dancing girls might try to sing or draw hoots and hollers from a drunken crowd. There was only a bar and a few tables surrounded by smoke from a cooking stove in the back room. Slocum thought he could detect the scent of burnt toast and potatoes, which meant there likely wouldn't be much of a crowd for meals either. The nameless place suited his needs just fine.

He felt better once got into his room and no longer had to carry those damn saddlebags everywhere. Once they were dropped into one corner and the pouch was tucked safely into his boot, he headed out again. Nobody greeted him on his way down. In fact, the man who'd given Slocum the key to the room barely even acknowledged he was there. The sole customer in the saloon was too drunk to lift his head and the girl who'd been sweeping the floor when he'd arrived had already wandered off to find another chore to do.

Perfect.

On his way back to the stable, Slocum heard a train rattle up to the depot. It rolled past those groups of men and their telescopes, stopped just long enough to restock its coal stores, and huffed away by the time he approached the stable's front door. It was locked, so he walked around to try the side door. Although that one protested a bit, it came open after a few more tugs. Inside, Slocum found the gelding he'd ridden across the desert. "Hello there, boy," he said in a warm tone. "Looks like you're feeling better." After looking over the cuts and scrapes to find they'd been nicely cleaned, he checked the trough for water. A feed bag had been left open next to it so the horse could nibble at the remaining oats inside. "Better than I am anyhow. Looks like you could use a good brushing. Even if I have the money to pay extra, there's no reason I can't do the job myself." Slocum quickly found a brush nearby and picked it up. "Not like I have anything better to do anyway."

The process of brushing the horse was a simple and familiar one. His muscles moved on their own accord and he went about the task without having to truly think about what he was doing. In fact, the labor proved to be relaxing in its simplicity. It wasn't long before he worked up a sweat, and when he stripped off his shirt, the stagnant air felt somewhat cool against his damp skin.

The more he moved, the more he sweated. And the more sweat rolled down his body, the cooler he got. Since he was in a stable, he didn't even have to worry about appearances or unpleasant odors. Horses weren't mindful of such things, which made Slocum's time in that stable even pleasanter.

When he finished brushing the horse, Slocum looked for a pitchfork to move some hay around. He'd just found one when he heard the front door rattle before it was pulled open. Reflexively, his right hand found its way to the .44 at his side. When he saw who entered the stable, he relaxed his grip but kept his hand where it was.

"Oh!" the blond woman said as she jumped back a bit. "I heard someone in here and thought it was Cam."

"He's the one who owns this place?" Slocum asked.

"He is. I must say, though, I'm much more pleased to find you here instead of him."

"And why's that?"

She took a few steps inside, paused, and then reached

behind her to pull the door shut. Sweat glistened on her skin as well, but not as much as Slocum's. Her long, straight blond hair was tousled by the wind and her skirts flapped around her thanks to a gust of wind from the door swinging into place. "Because I like the way you looked at me." She stalked toward him like a cat, clasping her hands behind herself to arch her back and display her proud, ample breasts. "When you first arrived and put your horse up . . . you looked at me."

"Would have been rude to look away," Slocum said as he approached her. "Considering how pretty you are, it would have been a downright shame."

"I could tell you were a gentleman when I first laid eyes on you."

Slocum stepped right up to her, placed his hands upon her hips, and pulled her in close. "Gentleman? You'd be the only one in this town with that opinion."

She leaned back in his grasp; not exactly pulling away but not exactly giving in either. "People around here have plenty of opinions. I don't have much use for them."

"Considering what I've heard about you, I don't blame you."

This was another way for Slocum to test the waters. This time, the waters were very warm indeed. The blond woman placed her hands upon his, guiding them up along the sides of her body until he could feel the smooth slope of her breasts. Easing his palms downward to take a slower tour of her waist and hips, she said, "I don't give a damn what they say about me. If I worried so much about all of that, I wouldn't have time to enjoy my life. When you've seen the sort of pain and misery I have, simple pleasures become very important. I can tell that you know what I mean." She moved her hands along the scars and old wounds scattered along Slocum's body like a roadmap of the very pain she'd just addressed.

He allowed his hands to do some wandering as well. She was easily a foot shorter than him, but when she looked up at Slocum, it was with eyes that commanded attention. Whoever this woman was, no matter how much of what he'd heard was true or not, she wasn't to be taken lightly. "What's your name?" he asked.

"With all you've heard, you were never told my name?"

"No. I was just told to steer clear of you."

As her hands drifted lower, she traced a line along the top of his belt and then slipped one hand between his legs to cup a growing erection. Her fingers moved deftly back and forth, stroking him in a way that sent chills through his entire body. "You're doing a bad job of steering clear, Mr. Slocum."

"I don't listen to all the talk either. Even if some of it bears some truth."

"You believe what they told you about me?"

"Some of it."

She shrugged and rubbed up and down along the length of his stiffening cock. Pressing her breasts against his chest, she said, "Did you hear I was accused of hurting someone?"

"I did, but didn't hear why you'd do such a thing. There are plenty of reasons to hurt someone." Slocum moved his hands from the sides of her breasts to her hips and then around to cup her backside. Reaching down a little farther allowed him to feel some of the heat between her upper thighs. "There's also plenty of reasons to give someone the benefit of the doubt."

"I thought you were going to say you could learn to trust someone," she whispered.

"Trust doesn't come easy," Slocum said in a matching whisper. "But we don't need all of that to enjoy a few simple pleasures."

She smiled widely and started tugging at his belt buckle. "My name is Vivienne."

Slocum began unfastening the hooks on the back of her dress until the upper portion of the garment fell away. Her breasts were firm in his hands. Her bare flesh had the texture of smooth cream. "From what I've heard, you're a bad girl, Vivienne."

"Well now," she said as she lowered herself to her knees in front of him. "I'll see what I can do to live up to that."

As Vivienne's lips wrapped around his penis, Slocum slid his fingers through her straight blond hair. Her head bobbed back and forth and her tongue pressed flat against the underside of his rigid member. When she quickened her pace, she started sucking and her hands reached up to slide against his bare stomach.

Slocum closed his eyes and took deep breaths. The pleasure she was giving him was quickly growing, and if he didn't make some concerted efforts, he could very well be led to a swift climax. But he had other plans for her, and before she led him too far down that particular road, he eased back.

They looked at each other, knowing all too well what was to come without a word passing between them. Vivienne was helped to her feet and then allowed Slocum to remove the dress from her body. Beneath it, she wore a simple white slip, which she slowly peeled off while Slocum removed his clothing. She undressed so as not to rob him of the show, and she made certain to turn at the right moments so he could see the curve of her taut buttocks as she spread the slip upon the fresh hay in another stall. After lowering herself to the ground, she leaned back and propped herself up with both arms while arching her back to put her proud bosom on display.

Slocum stood naked in front of her. His cock was hard as iron, and every fiber of his being wanted to take the woman in front of him. As he lowered himself to the floor, Vivienne opened her legs and placed one little hand upon the thatch of downy hair between them. Her fingers wandered over the lips of her pussy and she let out a low, trembling moan.

At that moment, Slocum didn't think about anything but her. He didn't care if the front door of the stable was opened and half the town marched inside. He didn't even care what this woman may have done in the past. He'd known plenty of killers and plenty of thieves. According to many lawmen out there, he was worse than either of those things.

"Simple pleasures," he said with a grin. "Can never have too many of those."

Spreading her legs even wider, she reached down to grab his cock with both hands and guide it toward her wet mound. "I cannot agree more," she said. Slocum fit perfectly into her pussy, and with a little thrust, he was fully inside her. Once again, Vivienne leaned back and propped herself up with her elbows. She watched him intently as he started pumping in and out of her. The expression on her face was almost as enthralling as the rivulets of sweat tracing little glistening lines down the front of her naked body.

Having started on his knees between her thighs, Slocum now lowered himself on top of her. Vivienne's legs wrapped around him. Her skin was smooth and her muscles were taut as bowstrings as she drew him in and held him there. Her muscles weren't the only things that were tight. Once again, Slocum was brought to the brink of a climax when he felt just how firmly she enveloped him when he drove inside her.

When she grabbed hold of his arms with both hands, Vivienne was breathing in quick gulps. Slocum tried to move, but she urged him to stay put. He recognized the flush in her cheeks and waited until the last possible second before easing out and then pounding into her again.

"Oh my God!" she shouted. Judging by the look on her face, the outburst was as much a surprise to her as it was to Slocum. She watched him with wide eyes as Slocum bucked between her legs until she climaxed. When her orgasm came, she lay back and spread her legs as wide as she could.

Vivienne turned her head and gripped the slip beneath her back as if she were trying to pull up the stable's floorboards. Eventually, the pleasure receded and she began wriggling out from under him.

Slocum moved to the side and was almost immediately shoved back toward the slip that marked their spot on the floor. "Where do you think you're going?" she asked with a wicked glint in her eye.

"Nowhere. I just—"

"Damn right, nowhere," she said. "I'm not through with you yet."

Slocum wasn't done with her either, but wasn't about to put a stop to whatever she intended on doing. Instead, he allowed her to roll him onto his back so she could straddle his hips and look down at him. Grinning from ear to ear, she bent at the knees and squatted down until she was low enough to reach for his cock. "That's it," she purred as she fit the tip of his erection between her pussy lips. "Right where you belong."

Vivienne eased all the way down, taking every inch of him inside. Slocum placed his hands upon her legs and let out a breath as she started to ride him. At first, Vivienne moved slowly. Then, she put her hands upon her knees and started bouncing faster. The feel of her wet lips gliding up and down along the length of his shaft was similar to the way her mouth had felt when she'd sucked him. Eventually, she brought herself all the way down so she could situate herself into a slightly different position.

"Considering this reception," Slocum said, "I'm amazed you're not regarded more fondly by the men I've spoken to."

"Men?" she grunted. "What men? All I've seen since I got to town were worried little hens flinching every time they heard news about that killer—Ellis Jaynes—and some boys dressed in their daddy's clothes pretending to be hard men. You're the first hard man I've met in this town."

Slocum wanted to make a wisecrack about her choice of words, but was diverted almost immediately by the sight of her on top of him. Vivienne sat astride his hips with her legs tucked in on either side of him. She placed her hands flat upon his chest and rocked slowly back and forth. Her breasts swayed to the rhythm of her body and her hair drifted lazily as she closed her eyes and savored the hardness sliding in and out of her.

Before long, Slocum could no longer hold back. He placed his hands upon her hips, a spot he already knew so well, and massaged her smooth flanks. Reaching around, he cupped her tight little ass and started pumping up into her. Vivienne took a deep breath and held on to it as she accepted him inside. Although she ground against him and wriggled every now and then, she was clearly enjoying the fact that he'd taken complete control. Eventually, she straightened up and placed her hands upon her own breasts to rub them as Slocum drove every inch of his cock between her legs. From there, she leaned back and reached behind to grab his legs for support.

From that angle, Slocum was treated to a generous view of her proud breasts and erect nipples, which were now pointed directly at the stable's roof. Her stomach rose and fell as her breathing became faster. She even pumped her hips in a quick rhythm to match his thrusts.

Soon, Slocum felt his own climax approaching. It swelled inside him like a gust of wind and he knew it would be powerful when it hit. He didn't have to wait long for that moment, and when it happened, he snapped his head back and gripped her hard enough for his fingertips to dig into her flesh. While he hadn't meant to be rough with her, Vivienne didn't seem to mind. She sat upright again and then placed her hands once more on top of his.

"I've had to wait a long time to feel that good," she said.

"Well, just give me a few moments to catch my breath,"

Slocum replied. "I'll make sure you won't have to wait nearly as long for the next go-around."

She curled up beside him with a hand resting upon his chest, patiently waiting for Slocum to regain some wind as a contented grin drifted across her face.

6

After a long day spent in the stables and a longer night in his rented room, Slocum drifted off to sleep in a lumpy bed that was too small to share with anyone. Vivienne wasn't upset when she left him that night. On the contrary, she politely came up with a short list of reasons why she couldn't stay and Slocum wasn't offended in the slightest.

Bright and early the following morning, Slocum woke up and walked downstairs for some breakfast. The saloon wasn't open for business quite yet, but the owner was already cleaning up the place. He was more than happy to whip up some griddle cakes and coffee for him. The meal tasted like it had been made by a barkeep instead of a cook, but there were plenty of griddle cakes to be had with more than enough butter and syrup to give them some flavor. When his belly was full, Slocum tipped his hat to the barkeep, settled his bill, and carried his saddlebags to the stable.

Vivienne was there, but so were the liveryman and the town's head lawman. Marshal spoke to the other man in hushed tones, casting a few stern glances in Slocum's direction before leading the other man outside and out of earshot.

"What's that about?" Slocum asked as he went to his horse's stall and picked up his saddle.

She had her sleeves rolled up and was using a pitchfork to pile hay into a corner. Even with her blond hair tied back and dirt smudging her face, she still stirred something inside him. Using the back of her hand to wipe some sweat from her forehead, she replied, "There's been some trouble in town. I'm surprised you didn't hear."

"Between the ruckus we caused and the sleep I fell into afterward, I didn't hear much."

"You might want to keep your voice down about that."

"Why?" Slocum asked. "Still worried about your reputation?"

If he'd been talking to anyone else in her situation, he might have watched his tongue before saying something like that. But Vivienne was a free spirit, and even though he didn't have trouble believing she'd committed a sin or two, she seemed to have a good handle on things. When she heard him say that, however, a wince tugged at the corners of her mouth that made Slocum wish he'd been a little more cautious with his words.

Slocum placed a hand on her shoulder and said, "Sorry if I struck a nerve. I really haven't heard much of anything since I saw you."

She smiled. "I didn't hear much about it until I left your room last night. And even then, I only heard because it involved some folks I know rather well."

"In a town this size, I'd imagine you know just about everybody."

"That might be true if they wanted to know me."

Once again, Slocum felt bad for sticking his foot in his mouth.

"One of the stable hands was killed. Cut up pretty bad," she continued. "Sheriff thinks it may have been in a fight."

"Is it anyone I might have seen while I was here?"

"Maybe. His name is Derrick. Came to town less than six

months ago all the way from Boston I think. He was always nice to me. Of course, he always wanted something more than just a how-do-you-do, but that's not uncommon."

"A woman looking like you must get used to that sort of thing." Slocum was glad to see the tired smile his compliment brought to Vivienne's face. The smile disappeared just as quickly as it had come when the sheriff and the liveryman stomped in through the front doors.

"Where were you last night?" Marshal asked. "Couldn't find hide nor hair of you."

"Didn't know I was on such a short leash," Slocum replied.

"Long as you're in my town, you'll be on any leash I please. For now, just stay put. Will I be able to find you in the same spot as before?"

It took every bit of restraint Slocum could muster to keep from knocking the lawman onto his ass. It took even more to keep from glaring at the sheriff in a way that would betray what was truly running through his mind. After a few tense moments, Slocum nodded and said, "Yeah. Same place."

"Good. I'll want to have a word with you soon." With that, the sheriff turned sharply around and headed outside.

The liveryman looked Slocum up and down, sputtered a few halfhearted syllables, and then rushed to catch up to the sheriff.

Their footsteps were still fading when Slocum turned back to his horse and continued strapping the saddle to its back.

"Well," Vivienne said, "at least we can spend a little more time together tonight since you'll still be here and all."

"Sorry, but I must be moving along."

"But . . . he just said you were to stay put."

"I heard what he said," Slocum replied. "Don't mean I have to abide by it."

At first, Vivienne seemed shocked to hear such a thing. Then, a little grin flickered across her face. "He's the sheriff. You're just gonna tell him one thing and then do another?"

"I suppose . . . if that's what you want to call it." After cinching in the last strap, Slocum nodded and said, "On the other hand, I don't suppose there's any other thing to call it. I tried to help by bringing that dead robber to him and damn near got tossed into jail for it. That sheriff of yours is a strutting little jackass who's too wet behind the ears to know how to get his job done. If he had any sense at all, he would have organized a posse to go after that Ellis Jaynes fella a long time ago. Instead, he sits back and waits for someone else to bring a killer down. For all we know, there's already more men hiring on new gunhands to terrorize the same stretch of road."

"If he'd formed a posse now to check on that," Vivienne asked, "would you have joined?"

"Probably. Too many times, I've been the only one that seems concerned about bringing a killer to justice or protecting those who were hurt by men like Jaynes. It ain't my lot in life to just ride around and do jobs for men who are too damn lazy, stupid, or cowardly to get their own hands dirty. I'll lend a hand where I can and help when it's needed, but I ain't about to do your sheriff's bidding and I sure as hell ain't gonna set aside my business just because some little asshole with a badge pinned to his shirt tells me to."

Vivienne approached him and took hold of his shirt so she could pull him down and plant a kiss onto his lips. When she was through, she said, "You don't care for lawmen very much, do you?"

"As a general rule, not as such. After you run across so many crooked ones, it spoils you on the rest. There have been a few that were good enough, but they seem to be in the minority."

"I know what you mean. I guess our sheriff isn't much for impressing. Do you think he's crooked?"

Now that the saddle was in place, Slocum checked his gear. Next came the saddlebags, which he draped across the animal's back, where they belonged. "I haven't seen anything to make me think he was crooked. I'd say he was just in over his head. No," he corrected himself. "More like too ignorant to know he was in over his head. Either that or proud. Whichever it is, I don't make it a habit to suffer men like that. If I had nothing else to do, I might stay just to see how this pans out. Since I've got my business to tend to, I suppose this means we'll be parting ways."

"Whatever you think about the sheriff," Vivienne said in a soft tone, "I would have liked you to stay for a while."

Slocum led his horse from the stall and took a peek out the front door. Since there were no lawmen in sight, he figured Marshal was blowing his smoke in the privacy of his own office. "You could come with me," he offered.

"I could . . . what?"

"Come with me. I'm headed to Mescaline, but you could catch a stagecoach or a train to wherever you like. Doesn't seem like you have much keeping you here apart from a lot of folks who don't think very highly of you. Trust me, I've been plenty of places filled with them that don't want me there. It's not worth your time to be in a place like that as opposed to . . . well . . . anywhere else."

"It's not that simple," she said.

"Actually, it is. Most things in life boil down to some pretty easy notions. Go or stay. Do or don't. It only gets complicated in the execution, but every now and then some things really are just a matter of making a decision. The hardest part is in going against everything that's come before. Why are you staying here?"

After not a lot of consideration, she replied, "Because it's where I wound up."

"You may be surprised how many folks have the same answer to that question. If you don't like where you're at, find somewhere else to be. That line of thinking has been serving me well for a number of years."

"I guess it simply doesn't serve me well enough to leave just yet. Thanks for the offer, though."

Slocum let go of his reins so he could step up to her, wrap his arms around her, and draw her close for a long, lingering kiss. As much as he wanted to stay with her at that particular moment, he let her go so he could collect his reins and push open the stable's door. "If the day comes, you don't need me to pick up and go."

"I'll keep that in mind. You'd best go before the sheriff comes back around to collect you."

Now that he was outside, Slocum climbed into his saddle and said, "He can watch me go and wave good-bye, as far as I'm concerned."

"If he asks about you, I'll say I don't know why you left or where you went."

"Tell him everything I told you. If he needs to find me so badly, all he needs to do to ride to Mescaline. Somehow I doubt he'll find the time to go so far out of his way." Then Slocum flicked his reins and got his horse moving toward the street. There wasn't any movement through Davis Junction at that moment, so he stood out like a single bump on a log as he made his way toward the edge of town. Since there weren't any trains approaching or leaving the station, every step the horse took echoed down the street and rattled between the dusty buildings.

As was often the way, Slocum felt himself leaning in more than one direction. One part wanted to just get out of town and continue with his life at his own pace. He'd stepped in and cleaned up a small mess for the sheriff, and that was just fine.

Another part wanted to take his time in leaving Davis Junction so he could be certain the sheriff *saw* him going. Granted, that was a petty part of himself that he wasn't very proud of, but it was there all the same. Marshal just struck him as one of those people who figured he deserved to have most everything handed to him on a platter and that folks would just step in line and do what he told them because they didn't have a choice. Respect had to be earned, however. Slocum knew that much after years of experience and fighting to earn his fair share. Good men chose the rough path and did their best to ride it while lending a hand to others along the way. They didn't puff out their chests and act like the lord of the manor. By riding slowly enough to make certain the sheriff or his deputy caught sight of him, Slocum would be making a statement. If possible, he might even be able to add to that statement by riding off with the lawman hollering like a crazy man at his back.

Thinking about watching that brought a wicked grin to Slocum's face. Of course, if he did everything that he'd thought about while grinning that way, he would have found a permanent home behind a set of bars a long time ago.

The final part of him was tempted to steer his horse back to the stable, put it up for another night, and see what he could do to help the sheriff clean up whatever mess Ellis Jaynes may have left behind. There was something to be said for the Good Lord having a reason for putting a man in a certain place at a certain time. Plenty of men had stepped up to help him in times of need, and it was only proper that he should return the favor whenever he could.

"Slocum!" the sheriff shouted from somewhere behind him. "Get back here!"

Slocum sighed and weighed his options one last time. He was just beginning to favor helping the sheriff when Marshal hollered, "You'd best be moving that horse to more suitable accommodations so you can plant your ass back into that room you rented! Otherwise there'll be hell to pay, damn it!"

"Some men never learn," Slocum grumbled as he snapped his reins and tossed a wave over his shoulder. "It always pays to be neighborly instead of a strutting, squawking asshole."

Slocum left Davis Junction and didn't look back.

7

Throughout the better portion of that day, Slocum had been waiting to hear a horse or two gallop to catch up to him so the town's sheriff could give him what for. If anything, he figured Marshal would be bent far enough out of shape that he would simply have to remind him about jurisdiction and authority and any of the other long words spouted by men like him. But the only thing Slocum heard was the rumble of iron horses riding the tracks spanning one end of the country to the other.

After a while, he wondered if he might catch sight of a thief masquerading as an Indian brave sitting on a high ridge somewhere. But he didn't see that either. All that filled Slocum's line of sight that day was flat terrain, sun-baked rocks, trails of smoke from steam engines, and the occasional clump of parched scrub bushes. Before long, even the trains were too far away to see or hear. Critters scattered as his horse rumbled by, seeking shelter in little caves or dens scratched out of the uncompromising ground.

As far as deserts went, Smoke Creek wasn't a large one. He could have circled around it while only adding a few days to his ride, but that involved passing through some terrain that was just a little more difficult to traverse. As long as he knew there was an end in sight, riding through a desert was actually not so bad. In fact, forging through a cauldron of heat and arid harshness did something to cleanse a man's soul. If Slocum had to ride more than one long day, he would have grudgingly picked one of those harder routes instead of the one that led straight to Mescaline. As it was, he'd committed himself to his course and was too stubborn to veer from it now.

The first time he'd come this way, he didn't have so many choices. He'd been riding scout for a small wagon train full of prospectors with their eyes set firmly on the mines scattered throughout Nevada. They'd lost a few horses, which made for a bad situation, and when one of the men decided to steal the savings of everyone else in the wagons so he could strike out for a new life, the situation turned bad. When Slocum had arrived in Mescaline back then, crawling in from the desert nursing a few wounds, things got even worse.

He'd been introduced to Jeremiah Hartley when the outlaw had tried to kill him just to prove that he made every decision in Mescaline, including who got to come in and who got to leave. Mescaline had been a little town far from the reaches of the law. Even if there were a few well-meaning sheriffs scattered throughout the other neighboring towns, their reach didn't extend far enough to help the people there. Hartley got to do what he pleased, and when a man as cruel as him was given that kind of leverage, it didn't bode well for anyone who got in his way.

Locking horns with Hartley hadn't been easy. In the end, however, Slocum was the one who walked away from it with his life and Hartley was dumped into a shallow hole. A fitting end for a man who'd created so much misery in an already miserable world.

The people in Mescaline had been grateful. They'd heaped their praises upon Slocum's shoulders and waved tearfully when he left. While Slocum wouldn't have minded reaping a bigger reward, he hadn't taken on Hartley for that. He'd done it because he simply had no tolerance for small men imposing their will upon good people. Also, he wasn't about to become a smaller man himself by staying around like a dog that had worn out its welcome just so he could lap up a bit more attention. On the other hand, being known as something other than a vagrant or stranger in a place could serve a man well.

Slocum did have business to conduct, and selling gold with someone who was playing straight was a much brighter prospect than trading with a man looking to put one over on someone. Also, there was Anna Redlinger. Slocum had spent plenty of nights with her while he'd been in Mescaline. They were nights a man dreamt about when he was forced to sleep alone on a bedroll beside a dying fire surrounded by all manner of vermin and inclement weather. Even after the night he'd spent with Vivienne, Slocum still had a smile to spare when he thought back to his time with Anna.

Any of those reasons would have been enough to bring him back to Mescaline. On top of that, he was also curious to see how the folks he'd befriended there were doing after they'd been given their lives back. Slocum was feeling downright cheery when he spotted the first angular shapes in the distance marking a spot where the desert gave way to civilization. Dusk was swiftly approaching and there was a mighty hunger gnawing at his belly.

Tapping his heels against his horse's sides, Slocum allowed the gelding to run as fast as it liked for the last stretch. With an animal as spirited as his, it was all Slocum could do to keep his grip on the reins as the horse charged toward Mescaline. When he pulled back on the leather straps, Slocum felt as if he was arriving in a cloud of dust like something that had rolled all the way down from a mountaintop. Unfortunately, there wasn't anyone there to appreciate his dramatic flair.

In fact, he couldn't see anyone there at all.

Slocum rode slowly down the street leading straight through the middle of town. Although the buildings on either side were vaguely familiar, none of them matched his memories of the place. Rather than take time to ponder the many ways he could have embellished things while thinking back on them, he steered toward the closest place that looked as if it could offer him a good meal. The place called Slim's had been there on his first visit, and if he remembered correctly, it served a fine cut of steak.

The smile on Slocum's face appeared for two reasons: hunger and the fact that Anna Redlinger had been working at Slim's when he'd first met her. The water trough in front of the place had recently been filled, so he tied the gelding there and walked inside.

Slim's was just as he'd remembered it. A dining room the size of a closet that was filled with the aromas of cooking meat. There was one other customer inside, so Slocum tipped his hat to him and found a seat at a table away from the front window.

The woman who stepped out from the kitchen was not Anna Redlinger. In fact, she was large enough to be two Anna Redlingers. She waddled in, wearing an expression that was neither a smile nor grimace, huffing as if every step was a trial in balance and stamina. The rounded sides of her plump figure brushed the tables and chairs she passed enough so that the other customer there had to grab his glass of water before it was knocked over.

"What can I get for you?" she asked as she trundled to a stop at Slocum's table.

"How about a steak?" he asked.

"Just served the last one. It's late for supper."

"Try telling that to my stomach," Slocum said good-naturedly although his comment was not received as such. Since the expression on the large woman's face hadn't changed, it was difficult to say if it was received at all.

Without moving any more than was absolutely necessary, she replied, "Too late for supper. No more steak."

"What do you have?"

"Coffee."

"Anything to eat?" Slocum asked in a monotone that was almost a perfect match to the large woman's.

"Pie."

"Anything with meat?"

Twisting her face into a disgusted expression, she asked, "You mean like meat pie?"

If Slocum had had a white flag to wave, he would have surrendered the conversation right then and there. "Yeah," he sighed. "Meat pie. That's exactly what I mean."

"I'll go check."

"You do that."

She waddled back to the kitchen, leaving Slocum to wonder why the hell he'd bothered coming back to Mescaline. His curiosity was so far gone he could barely recall what it felt like. As for putting some distance between himself and Davis Junction, there was a perfectly good desert out there with caves that were more hospitable. Any other reasons he might have had slipped his mind altogether.

The big woman's steps as she returned to his table sounded like someone dragging a dead body over the floorboards. "We got a few pieces left," she grunted.

Slocum looked up at her and asked, "Of what? Meat pie?"

"Yes."

He blinked, wondering if she was joking. It didn't take much to see that she probably didn't know how to do such a thing with anybody. He might even go so far as to say that the severe lines on her face, like so many cuts in an oversized lump of clay, weren't made to express anything but the frumpy expression she showed him now. "I'll try it," he said. "Thanks very much."

She shrugged off his gratitude and shuffled back to the

kitchen. A few minutes later, she came back with a plate in one hand and a glass of water in the other. "I warmed it on the stove for a bit. Brought you something to drink. You want anything asides from water, it'll cost extra."

"Water is fine." Slocum leaned forward and drew in a long breath through his nose. The scents he inhaled brought a smile to his face. He looked down at the plate and saw it was covered in a generous portion of meat, brown gravy, some carrots and peas, as well as several chunks of potato within a flaky pie crust. "What kind of meat is that?" he asked.

"Beef and a few scraps of lamb. Had a farmer sell off his livestock on account of he was stupid."

"Stupid for selling?"

"Stupid for dragging livestock through a damn stretch of desert. Anything else I can get for you?"

"No, ma'am. This will do me just fine."

"Suit yerself. I'll be in back if you need me."

Slocum dug into the meat pie with the fork that had been wedged under his helping. It was rich and flavorful. If he didn't purposely slow himself down, he might have cleaned his plate before the rotund woman made her way to the kitchen. Even though the pie wasn't heated all the way through, it was still warm enough to suit his needs. To be honest, he would have downed his portion as well as another if she'd brought it to him cold.

It wasn't until he came up for air that Slocum realized he was being watched. The only other customer in the place had a face resembling a rock that had been stuck to the desert floor since before any man had dared to cross it. Deep lines etched into his cheeks extended all the way up to his eye sockets. Like many locals in such a dry climate, he looked like he wouldn't break a sweat if he was standing at the edge of a fiery lake in the bowels of hell. When he looked at Slocum, however, he might as well have been examining something dredged up from that very same lake.

Smiling in a way that he knew was showing a good portion of the meal he was enjoying, Slocum said, "Howdy."

The older man, who could have been triple Slocum's age, didn't return the greeting. He sat there, eyeing him carefully like an old vulture waiting for a wounded jackrabbit to stop kicking.

More than happy to focus on his meal, Slocum continued scooping bites of the pie into his mouth. It was amazing how much brighter a man's outlook could become after his belly was appeased. His mood improved even more as he washed down some of his dinner with water that was as cool as the bottom of a dark well.

"You from around here?" the old man asked.

The question came after Slocum had taken a few more bites. He was enjoying his food so much that he wasn't thinking of anything else. When he looked up from his plate, Slocum found the old buzzard looking just as he'd left him. "No, sir," he replied. "Just here to conduct some business."

"What kind of business?"

"I'm looking to see Ed Leigensheim. Does he still have an office here in town?"

The old man nodded. "He does. What business you got with him? Looking to sell something?"

"I am."

"You'll have to wait until tomorrow. His place is closed for the day."

"Figured as much," Slocum said. "It's a bit late for business. I'm in the market for a place to stay, though. Is the Three Star still down the street?"

The old man didn't nod. His eyes narrowed as he replied, "It is. Sounds to me like you been here before."

"I have, but it's been a while."

"I reckon it has." Leaning forward as if that extra inch or two would allow him to see more, the old man said,

"There's a familiar look about you. When were you here last?"

"It's been some time."

"Back in the days when Jeremiah Hartley was runnin' this town?"

The smile that had been put onto Slocum's face by the meal slowly dropped away. He set his fork down and took a sip of water that felt as sobering as if it had been splashed onto his face. "Yeah," he said. "Right around then."

When the old man grinned, it was a humorless expression that barely caused one corner of his mouth to creak upward. His eyes were sharp as nuggets of coal that had been scraped to a point and baked to a hardened sheen. "That'd make you John Slocum."

"You got that much from what I told you?"

"I says you have a familiar look," the old man replied. "I just now recall where I remember seeing you. What the hell are you doing back in Mescaline?"

"I wasn't aware that I'd worn out my welcome."

"Now you know." The old man pushed his chair back, took the napkin from his lap, and then slammed it down upon the table. "It's best if you just finish yer meal, drink yer water, and be on yer way."

Whenever Slocum put his neck on the line to help someone, it was mainly because he knew he was doing the right thing. He didn't risk his life so others would be indebted to him, but a bit of gratefulness went a long way to see him through tough times. He couldn't help but think about the grateful smiles he'd seen on so many faces just before he'd left Mescaline the last time.

"What's brought this on, old man?" he asked. "I just got here."

"Last time you was here, you did enough," the old man told him. "If yer looking for a hero's welcome now that you dragged yourself back into town, you ain't gonna find it.

I recall what you did. I recall how you escorted Jeremiah Hartley straight to hell, which is why I'm givin' you this friendly piece of advice. Leave town. Now."

With that, the old man left the restaurant. He didn't say another word and didn't cast another glance in Slocum's direction.

There were still a few more bites of pie on Slocum's plate, and he'd be damned if he was going to let them go to waste. When he ate them, however, he wasn't as cheerful as he'd been during the first couple of mouthfuls. He'd finished up most of the meal and was using the side of his fork to scrape up the gravy and extra pieces of crust and vegetables when the big woman emerged from the kitchen amid the now familiar sound of heavy, shuffling steps.

Rather than wait for her to cross the room, Slocum put his fork on top of his plate, swallowed the last gulp of water from his glass, and got up to take those things to her.

Accepting the dirty plate that was handed over, she asked, "Is that true?"

"You mean what the old man was saying?" Slocum asked.

"I mean about you being John Slocum."

"It's true."

"Then you don't owe a dime for your supper."

"I appreciate that, ma'am."

Before he could say another word, she told him, "I didn't see you up close back when you were here last, so I didn't recognize you now. All I saw during the last days of Jeremiah Hartley was a whole lot of blood in the sand and shooting in the streets. I kept my head down and only peeked out to make sure it was safe to step into the daylight again."

Slocum remembered plenty more during those days that didn't involve shooting, but wasn't about to correct her.

"Plenty of folks here remember them days," she continued. "Most are grateful to you. Most don't hold you accountable for what happened afterward since you left."

"What did happen?"

"You need to go," she said, sidestepping his question as clumsily as if she'd tried to step around a loose floorboard. "Go right now and don't come back, you hear?"

"Can't you just—"

"Go! That's all I got to say to you!"

And so . . . Slocum went.

8

Slocum stepped outside with questions swirling inside his head fast enough to upset the food he'd so recently eaten. What settled even worse was the fact that he felt even less welcome in Mescaline than he had in Davis Junction. Questions and possibilities drifted through his mind, none of which he could put to rest since none of the few folks he'd seen were ready to say more than a couple words on the subject.

His horse waited at the trough, looking refreshed after having drunk a good portion of the water in front of him. The gelding nudged Slocum's hand as he held it out to him, snuffing calmly as Slocum patted the side of his neck. Before Slocum could climb into the saddle or take the reins, a pair of figures rounded a corner and walked toward the little restaurant. Thanks to the torches that had been lit on that side of the street, he could also see the angry faces they wore.

"Easy, boy," Slocum said to the horse. "Things look like they might get a bit rough."

The two men who approached were about the same

height. Slocum guessed they were both a hair shorter than him, which wouldn't make a lot of difference since they were armed with at least one pistol and a shotgun apiece. They held their shotguns ready and in front of them, but for the moment, the barrels were aimed at the dirt just ahead of their feet.

"What's your business here, mister?" one of them asked. He was slightly taller than the other one and wore a bowler hat. His partner scowled beneath the brim of an old Stetson.

Slocum stepped away from his horse, but made sure he was within a short distance of the rifle in his saddle's boot. For the time being, he was confident he wouldn't need any more than what was already at his disposal. "Why's everyone so interested in that?" he asked. "I've been in town less than an hour and have already been questioned a few times. Didn't Mescaline used to be a friendly place?"

"Yeah," the shorter fellow said. "Used to be. But you probably know all about that."

"Shut up, Matt," the one in the bowler said. Shifting the finger he'd been pointing toward Slocum, he added, "As for you, mister. You ain't wanted around here."

"So let me guess," Slocum said in a tired voice. "You want me to leave?"

"Oh, you'll be leaving all right. Feet first."

Both men stood side by side. They spread out and began stalking forward with cruel intentions written across ugly faces.

"What's the meaning of this?" Slocum asked. "You gonna tell me what this is about?"

"You're John Slocum?"

"That's right."

"Then you should know damn well what this is about."

"How about you enlighten me?" When neither of the other men responded, Slocum squared his shoulders to them and placed his hand less than two inches above his holstered .44.

"If you want to steam ahead without explaining yourselves, that's fine by me. I can ask my questions to whoever shows up at your funeral."

That stopped both men dead in their tracks. They were well within the serviceable range of their shotguns, but didn't seem as keen to use them as they'd been scant moments ago. The one who had been called Matt looked to the one wearing the bowler as he became increasingly less comfortable in his own skin.

"I heard about him, Luke," Matt said. "If this is John Slocum . . ."

"If this is John Slocum, then we're about to become rich. Both of us. Now shut up and do like we planned."

"If you planned on dying," Slocum warned, "you're both going about it the right way."

Both men planted their feet. Matt was still fidgety, but held his ground.

Luke tightened his grip on his shotgun, but still wasn't ready to bring it up to bear. "You come here for Mr. Dawson?"

Slocum slowly shook his head. "Don't even know who that is."

"Well, he sure knows you."

One thing that Slocum appreciated about nervous men with guns was their tendency to talk more than they should. A fearful soul often made for loose lips or itchy britches and these two had both. While Luke couldn't stop talking, Matt couldn't stop nervously shifting from one foot to the other.

"Mr. Dawson's got a standing order," Luke said. "It says he'll pay for any word that John Slocum is in this state. If'n anyone by that name sets foot in Mescaline, he's to be shot on sight."

"Those are harsh words," Slocum said.

"Damn straight."

"I would have thought a man with that kind of hatred for

me would have sent more than the two of you to get the job done."

"We're more than enough, mister," Luke boasted.

"If you're certain about that, I'll give you a chance to prove it."

Although Matt had stopped fidgeting so much, he'd drawn himself tighter than a bowstring, which wasn't exactly a good thing. Luke ground his teeth together, thinking so hard about what he should do next that smoke was about to come from his ears.

Slocum had given them so much slack for one reason. If there was anyone backing their play, odds were best that those other men would make themselves known right about now. Nobody stepped up on their behalf, however. In fact, there was hardly anyone to be seen on either side of the street.

"There must be more," Slocum prodded. "Something that would make two men like yourselves risk your lives on such a fine night as this."

"Three thousand dollars," Luke replied.

Slocum let out a low whistle. "All of that for me? Why don't you take me to have a word with this Mr. Dawson and we can split the money?"

"D-Don't work that way," Matt sputtered. "It's three thousand for your body. Dead body, that is."

"Ah," Slocum said. "There's always a catch."

Even with this stalling, Slocum saw no trace of backup coming. Even someone positioned on high ground somewhere would have taken a shot by now. The instincts that had seen him through tougher scrapes than this one told him there would be nobody on a rooftop. Just to be safe, Slocum had made sure to be far enough away from the few crackling torches along the street to make it difficult for anyone to get a clear shot. What puzzled him most was the lack of spectators. Even the purest souls tended to get curious when a fight was brewing within earshot.

"Can I ask why he wants me dead?"

Both of the other two men looked at Slocum as if he'd just sprouted horns. Surprisingly, it was Matt who told him, "You know why. Otherwise, you ain't John Slocum."

"That's who he is, all right," Luke said. "I'd stake my life on it."

"And your life is exactly what you're about to lose," Slocum said in what was to be the last warning he'd give either of them.

Both men stood rooted to their spots with shotguns in hand, licking their lips in anticipation of what was to come. Whether they were anxious to pull their triggers or just thinking about how they could spend three thousand dollars, Slocum couldn't say. What he knew for certain was that they weren't about to back down.

Rather than watch their eyes, Slocum paid close attention to their arms and hands. Luke and Matt were too skittish for their faces to tell him much, but they would have to tense their arms if they intended to bring up their shotguns. His money was on Luke being the first to break the standoff, and Slocum didn't have to wait long before he was proven right.

Luke tightened his grip on the shotgun and lifted it to angle the barrel so it would point at Slocum. In the time it took for the shotgun to shift a few degrees in his direction, Slocum reached for the .44 at his hip and wrapped his fingers around the pistol's comfortable grip. He kept his body still and his eyes fixed upon his target while going through motions that were so well practiced they flowed like finely oiled machinery.

As soon as he cleared leather, Slocum pivoted the .44 and squeezed off a quick shot. When that round hissed past his head, Luke reacted by firing a shot of his own. The shotgun roared with a plume of fire that illuminated him, Matt, and a good portion of the street. Most of the buckshot dug into the ground while some of it chipped at the edges of the water trough Slocum's gelding had nearly drained. Slocum might have been grazed as well if he hadn't already launched himself to one side.

As he sailed through the air, Slocum kept his aim on Luke. Matt was frozen in place, so Slocum let him stand there like a sapling and shake in the wind. He pulled his trigger again, firing too quickly to be very accurate, but luck smiled upon him and he clipped Luke's upper arm to spin him around as blood sprayed from the newly opened wound.

"Shoot, damn you!" Luke hollered as he staggered back. "Or I'll shoot you myself!"

Matt blinked once and turned upon Slocum like a mad dog. The change in his expression was jarring as he suddenly became a man capable of ending another's life. He made a quick adjustment to his stance and fired the shotgun from hip level. Not known for its accuracy under the best circumstances, the shotgun roared to shatter one of the windows across the street. Slocum and everything else in front of that smoking barrel were unharmed.

Slocum landed on his side and he fired another quick shot as he got his legs beneath him to send both other men scattering for cover. By the time he was upright again, Matt had found a post to stand behind and Luke had chosen to squat behind a barrel.

The post was barely wide enough to provide cover for a mouse, which meant most of Matt was in plain sight. Slocum took aim and sent a round through the meat in the back of Matt's leg. He yelped in pain and dropped like a load of bricks, allowing his shotgun to slip from his hands and land in the dirt nearby.

Luke was well hidden behind his barrel, and when he saw his partner fall, he stretched out both arms to point the shotgun at Slocum. He wasn't able to aim in that fashion, but still looked like he might get close enough to do some real damage. Slocum ducked down and hurried away to clear a path by the time Luke pulled his trigger. The shotgun roared again, sending its smoky payload in a wide arc through the air. Another window shattered and Slocum's gelding whinnied, but no blood was spilled.

"That was your second barrel," Slocum said.

"The hell it was!" As he shouted back, Luke leaned out from behind his cover and sighted along the top of a pistol he must have drawn since finding his hiding spot. As Slocum guessed, that shot was wild and much too panicked to come close to hitting him. The bullet hissed through the air several yards above its intended target to sail into the inky night sky. Slocum had gotten what he was after, so he drilled through the barrel where Luke was hiding with a careful shot that caused him to jump into the open quicker than a scalded dog.

"What are you waiting for, damn it?" Luke shouted to the man still writhing on the ground. "You still got a barrel left and a gun at yer side. Use 'em!"

"I'm hit, Luke!"

"You dyin'?"

"No," Slocum replied. "He's not dying."

Matt looked up at him with wide, terrified eyes. "How do you know?"

"Because," Slocum replied, "if I'd wanted you dead, you'd be dead. You've just got a flesh wound in the leg. A blind man could see as much from where I stand."

Matt wriggled like a worm on a hook until he could get a better look at his bloody leg. The back section of his jeans was ripped to shreds from the glancing shot and the edges of the tear were blackened by the bullet's passing. Blood poured from his gaping wound, but not enough to cause much concern. Even so, Slocum pointed out, "You'll need to get that stitched up. You're losing plenty of blood."

"Go to hell!" Matt shouted. "You're the one that shot me!"

"And you're the one that came at me when all I wanted was some fresh air after a good meal."

"He's only got one shot left," Luke said to his partner. "I counted. We can still bring him down."

"You're full of surprises, Luke," Slocum said. "I would never have thought you could count."

Matt started pulling himself toward his shotgun, dragging the weight of his body as if both legs had been blown off at the knees. He started to crawl, which gave him some bit of pain. He didn't have far to go, so his dramatic display was short-lived. When he got to the shotgun, he placed one hand over it and held it there.

"What are you waiting for?" Luke demanded. "Pick it up!"

"What about you, big man?" Slocum asked. "You've got a gun already in hand. You gonna put it to use, or are you content to stand back and bark orders at someone else?"

Luke ignored Slocum completely and snarled at his partner, "Pick up that damn shotgun! He can't shoot both of us!"

"That's right," Slocum said. "I can't. But I can get one of you for certain. And when I do get that one, I can promise it won't be a flesh wound or anything like the little nicks I've handed out so far. I'll burn a hole through your face that'll empty what little brains you have onto the street for all of Creation to see." Slowly casting his glare back and forth between the other two men, he added, "Which of you is gonna step forward for that?"

After a second or two to consider it, Matt eased his hand away from the shotgun. In his haste to distance himself from the weapon he'd dropped, he was able to climb to his feet and grit his teeth through the pain he felt when using his wounded leg to support himself. "I'm through with this," he squeaked. "I . . . I never wanted to go about it like this in the first place."

Slocum nodded and focused most of his attention on Luke. If Matt made a move for the shotgun, he'd see it from the corner of his eye, but he wasn't too worried about that one anymore. "So it's down to you and me then," he said to Luke. "You still have the advantage, seeing as how you've got more bullets to fire. I've only got the one. Guess I'd better make it count."

Even though Luke didn't say a word, Slocum could read plenty in his eyes. They moved in quick, jerking twitches within their sockets. Surely he was pondering the image of his life ending in a red, pulpy mist exploding from the back of his skull. Soon, his face started to twitch. When Slocum saw Luke's gun hand tremble, he knew the fight was all but over.

"Who's this Mr. Dawson?" Slocum asked.

Luke's hand had stopped trembling, but every muscle in his face was tightened with the effort of keeping it steady.

Slocum was ready to fire at any moment. His gun wasn't pointed at Luke, which was his intention. If a man was absolutely certain he was about to die, he'd lash out like any animal after being backed into a corner. But if he thought there was a chance to live, no matter how slim, he became much more susceptible to reason.

"Whoever he is," Slocum said, "he must be pretty important for you to lay down your life this way."

Sweat broke out onto Luke's brow, glinting with reflected moonlight and a few stray beams from a nearby torch.

Slocum lowered his pistol until his arm hung loosely at his side. It made him appear less threatening even though it would still only take a slight effort for him to aim and fire. "If you're set on earning that three thousand dollars," he said, "then make your move. Otherwise, drop that pistol and walk away."

"You'll shoot me no matter what," Luke spat.

Slocum shook his head. "It's like I said before. All I wanted was some fresh air after my meal. I've had it. Whatever happens next is up to you."

Now that he was given a choice, Luke relaxed a bit. As

he regained some of his composure, a bit of his fighting spirit came along with it.

Recognizing the glint that drifted into Luke's eyes, Slocum cocked his head slowly to one side. A wolf baring its teeth to an approaching rival angled its head in much the same manner and with similar results.

Luke knew right away that he wasn't about to get the drop on the man in front of him. Even more, he could tell he'd already taken one too many steps in the wrong direction. Just like a lesser animal that saw the warning snarl from that wolf, he changed direction right quick.

"All right," Luke said. "I'll go."

"Leave the pistol," Slocum warned.

Having already admitted defeat, Luke dropped his weapon without hesitation.

Pointing a finger at Matt without taking his eyes off Luke, Slocum said, "I haven't forgotten about you. Leave that shotgun where you dropped it along with any other guns you're carrying."

"B-But them are my guns," Matt said meekly. "I . . . I own 'em."

"You want them back, come and find me some other time. I have a feeling we'll be crossing paths again."

Slocum put just enough of an edge into his tone to make both men carry out the orders they'd been given with haste. Matt was in such a hurry to leave that he didn't even remember he'd been injured until he made it to the corner. Luke helped his partner along, but not without a steady tongue-lashing to go with it.

As he collected the guns that had been left behind, Slocum waited for any sign that there were more gunmen to worry about. Although the street remained silent for the time being, he didn't fool himself into thinking it would stay that way for long.

9

The Three Star Hotel was where Slocum had stayed the last time he was in town. Back then, it was a modest little place run by a family who'd just gotten started and had thrown everything they had into maintaining their business. The rooms were small, but clean. The meals served were tasty and stuck to a man's bones. Most important, the beds were a hell of a lot better than sleeping on a bedroll in the middle of the desert. Slocum headed there now because he simply couldn't recall the name of any other hotels in Mescaline.

On his way there, he felt more and more eyes staring at him from behind darkened windows and shadowy doorways. After having to endure a long day's ride and the scuffle in the street, he no longer gave a damn who was watching as he, his horse, and a bundle of recently acquired firearms made their way to the three-story building near the center of town. The outside of the Three Star was much fancier than he recalled, and there were plenty of lanterns burning within. Slocum tied his horse to a post, entered the hotel, and walked up to a desk where a tall, frail-looking woman stood with a pencil already in hand.

"Can I . . . help . . ." The woman's question trailed off as her eyed narrowed into a harsh squint. She stared intently at the man that had just walked in from the darkness before whispering, "John? Is that you?"

Slocum nodded and gave her a tired smile. "It is." When he'd started talking, Slocum couldn't remember her name. Just seeing the woman's narrow features and warm eyes brought her right back to the front of his thoughts. "It's . . . Margaret, right?"

Her smile had been there before, but now it positively beamed. "That's right! I didn't think you'd remember."

"You remembered me."

"Well, after what happened when you were in town last time, it would be next to impossible to forget you."

"This time is shaping up to be fairly interesting as well," Slocum said. "I'd be surprised if you hadn't heard the commotion."

"I did hear something, but I guess I just thought it could have been some drunks or the like."

Slocum could tell she had more to say on the matter, but he was too tired to press. Instead, he told her, "I could use a room. Do you have anything on the third floor?"

"No, but I have plenty of nice rooms on the second."

"Sounds fine. Something away from the stairs if you've got it. I'd also like a good view of the street."

She smiled again nervously. "Now that sounds familiar."

"Yeah, I suppose I did have to watch my back and just about every other part of me when Hartley started going on his tear."

To anyone who'd lived in Mescaline during those days, mentioning that name was more than enough to send a chill down their spine. Whether it was followed by anger, fear, or sadness, the chill worked its way through Margaret's body and made her avert her eyes. When she looked back at him, she forced herself to remain steady.

"It's good to have you back, John. What brings you to Mescaline?"

"I found myself in Nevada and had some business to conduct," Slocum told her. "I figured since I'm on good terms with folks around here, I'd stop by, conduct my business, and see how everyone was doing since I left."

Margaret nodded stiffly.

"I am still on good terms with folks around here, right?" he asked.

Her lips pressed tightly together but soon curled into a genuine, albeit weary, smile. "I can only speak for myself and a few others, but I can say you're definitely a welcome sight. Always will be."

He looked across the desk at her, studying her stance as well as her face. He wanted to ask about the two men that had sought him out and why nobody had bothered to step foot outside to watch, lend a hand, or even take a look at what was left behind after the smoke cleared. The law may have left a bad taste in his mouth fairly recently, but the fact that no authority of any sort came along during or after the fight outside the restaurant was just plain odd.

Then there was the name he'd heard from Luke and Matt. Mr. Dawson.

Slocum would have bet a pretty penny that he'd get a reaction from Margaret if he dropped that name right now. Since he was certain the reaction wouldn't have been a very good one, he held his tongue. Slocum knew the woman had been through plenty and that didn't take into account whatever had come to pass since he'd left the first time. He wasn't in the mood to rattle her again just so he could put a question or two to rest. Considering how important this Dawson fellow was and the fact that shots had already been fired in his name, Slocum was certain he'd find out more about him without having to wait very long.

"Is there anything else I can do for you?" Margaret asked.

"Yes," Slocum said as he took the key she handed to him. "Tell me you're still the one that cooks breakfast for the guests. I'd cross the desert on my hands and knees if your biscuits and gravy were waiting for me."

Her shoulders lowered as if she'd finally let out a breath that she'd been holding for the better part of a week. "I'll have a hot plate waiting for you in the morning, along with a fresh pot of coffee."

"Sounds perfect."

"Is there anything else I can do for you, John?"

There was plenty, but Slocum decided to let it wait for another day. "I'd just like some sleep. Can I put my horse up in the back like before?"

"Yes. There should be fresh oats just inside the door."

He tipped his hat to her and went outside. The moment the cool night air washed across his face, Slocum felt like he was once again on display. More than that, he felt exposed from several angles. The shadows were so thick in several sections of the street that just about anything could be hiding in them. A few torches sputtered in various spots, but they wouldn't do much do keep back any predators that wanted to remain out of sight. There were plenty of rooftops where someone could make their perch, but Slocum's gut was still telling him he was safe.

At least . . . as safe as he could be in a town containing men who wanted to see him dead. He chuckled to himself as he took the gelding's reins and led it around the hotel. If he tried to avoid any place where people wanted to do him harm, Slocum would be confined to a very small patch of land somewhere in an Alaskan snow field.

Some men wanted to kill him because of some old score to settle.

Some wanted to collect one of a few rewards that had been placed on his head. Thinking along those lines, Slocum added Dawson's three thousand dollars to that list.

And some men just wanted to test themselves against John Slocum because they knew some other gunmen had lost a fight to him. Young outlaws were always looking to add a notch to their belt or polish their reputation, and Slocum didn't have the inclination to sort through the number of times he'd been fired upon for such a paltry reason.

He'd reached the little barn behind the hotel that was used as a livery stable for the hotel's owners and guests. The door wasn't locked, so he pulled it open to reveal an old carriage with wheels that could have been fixed if a talented blacksmith rolled up his sleeves and pounded them out for about a week and a half. Spiders and mice had claimed the carriage's interior. Fortunately, that dirty old relic was on one side of the barn and the trio of horse stalls were on the other.

Slocum led his gelding to one of the two unoccupied stalls and rummaged around for a feedbag. He found one hanging on the edge of the stall's door, and when he glanced back to the front door, he found a bag of oats sitting right where Margaret had said it would be. He approached the oats, stooped down to pick them up, and saw a flurry of movement just outside the barn.

Reflexes brought Slocum's hand to his holster even before he got a look at who was rushing toward him.

The figure moved silently upon feet covered in flat shoes. The dark brown cotton dress draped around the tall, lithe figure made more noise as it flapped in the breeze than the young woman who raced into the barn. She charged at Slocum, recklessly throwing herself at him without an ounce of concern for the pistol he'd almost drawn from the holster at his side.

"Oh my God," she sighed as she wrapped her arms around the back of his neck and pressed herself up against him. "It *is* you, John!"

"Anna," Slocum said in a voice muffled by the woman who was now clinging to him. "I meant to find you, but I just got into town."

Anna Redlinger held his face in her hands and leaned back a little to get a better look at him. Her face was just as pretty as he remembered—framed by plenty of flowing, light brown hair. A pert little nose sat at the center of her features like a single button placed upon a lovingly tailored doll. Her lips formed a little bow just beneath it and were colored as if they'd been rubbed by freshly picked strawberries.

"Are you all right?" she asked. "I heard there was trouble. I heard shots. What happened?"

"I'm not hurt," he said. "You heard the shots?"

"Of course I did. This isn't exactly a rowdy town."

"How come nobody came out when they were fired?" Slocum asked. Before he could ask his next question, Anna pulled him in closer and pressed her mouth upon his lips in a long, powerful kiss filled with more urgency than passion. The instant he tasted the familiar flavor of her, Slocum wrapped his arms around Anna's waist and felt her thin frame melt against him.

Several parts of his body responded as if it had only been a matter of hours since the last time he'd felt Anna's naked flesh beneath his searching hands. However, he forced himself to take her slender arms in his grip and push her back a few steps. She looked at him with surprise and a hint of fear when he snapped, "What the hell are you doing?"

"I was worried about you, John."

"There wasn't a soul out there when I faced those other two men. Where were you that you could see what was going on so well?"

"I couldn't see it. Otherwise, I would have found you sooner."

"How did you find me at all?" he asked.

"Bess told me you were at her restaurant. Don't you remember? That was the place where we first met each other."

Slocum let go of her, suddenly feeling a bit of shame for handling her so roughly. "Yeah," he sighed. "I remember. It's been a long night. Sorry about speaking so cross to you just now."

Although she rubbed her arms where he'd grabbed her, Anna quickly stopped so as not to make him feel any worse and said, "I understand. Are you sure you're all right?"

"I'm fine. Those two that came after me couldn't hit the broad side of a barn if their lives depended on it."

"That was Matt and Luke. They probably thought they could sneak up and shoot you in the back while you were still eating."

"So you know them?" Slocum asked.

She nodded. "Not very well, but I've seen them here and there. Usually, they just collect on debts and such for Mr. Dawson."

"I've heard that name a lot since I've been in town. Who the hell is Mr. Dawson and why is he connected to a couple of assholes who tried to take a shot at me when I was still picking supper from my teeth?"

"It's best you don't worry about him," she replied. "Just do whatever you need to do quickly and put this town behind you."

Slocum shook his head. "I'm not about to do that. Not after all the trouble I went through to clean these streets the first time."

"You did more than any of us had a right to ask. As for what happened after you left . . . that's not your fault."

"Whose fault was it? What the hell happened anyway?"

Outside, a horse rode up to the hotel and came to a stop. Since Anna was already mostly inside the barn, Slocum pulled her the rest of the way inside and wrapped his arms around her to keep her in place. Although Anna struggled a little, it was mostly to regain her footing instead of genuinely trying to get away from him.

"Shh," Slocum whispered almost directly into her ear. Opening the door a crack, he used a finger to point at the rider that was now climbing down from the horse. "Do you know who that is?"

"No," she replied. "Can't hardly see from here."

There was a chance that the rider was just another weary soul looking for a place to rest after coming in from the desert. Then again, judging by the way he stomped toward the Three Star's front door, it seemed more likely that he had some manner of urgent business inside.

"Stay put," Slocum whispered. "I want to take a look."

"No," Anna said insistently. She planted her feet and positioned himself in front of him to act as a barrier between Slocum and the outside world. "He's probably got something to do with those other two who came after you. It might even be Matt or Luke looking to take another shot at you."

"I know. That's why I'm going to get closer and see for myself."

Anna started to protest, but Slocum quieted her the same way she'd quieted him a few moments ago. Pulling her in, he gave her a kiss that quickly turned into a lingering, passionate embrace. Their hands moved along each other's bodies as if they already knew right where they wanted to go. Her arms cinched in tighter around him and she even moaned softly as Slocum's tongue found its way into her mouth. When his hands brushed against her hips, she pulled in an expectant breath only to let it out when he pulled away.

"Come with me," she said.

"Stay here. I may take you up on that offer when I come back."

"If you come back."

"After all that happened before," Slocum said, "you think someone can just ride up and kill me so easily?"

"This isn't like when Jeremiah Hartley was here. This is something different."

"Care to tell me about it?"

Reluctantly, she replied, "Come with me right now and I will."

"Sorry, but the longer I wait right now, the less chance I have of getting there and back without being seen. You sit tight and don't make a sound. Be ready to move the moment

I come back. Is there a way we can go that doesn't take us past that hotel?"

"Yes."

"Then be ready to show it to me real soon." With that, Slocum gave her a playful swat on the backside as he left the barn with quick, silent steps.

He stayed low and moved forward swiftly. Slocum kept his chin up and was always careful to stay in as much darkness as he could find. The Three Star was a good size and he could see plenty of movement behind some of the windows that were still lit by candles or lanterns within their rooms. Most of them were on the third floor, which made sense because apparently those were all rented for the night.

It didn't take long for him to get to the main building, but Slocum felt a knot in his stomach as if he was about to be discovered. He reached the side of the hotel and did his best not to make any noise as he caught his breath. In those moments, he could hear bits of conversation from inside.

The rider stood at the front door and had either left it open or was so close to it that his voice carried outside. Of course, it didn't help that he spoke in a bellowing tone.

"What room is he in?" the rider asked.

Margaret answered in a firm, solid tone. "He's one of *my* guests. I don't answer to you."

"The hell you don't, bitch. Tell me what I want to know before I slap that ugly face of yours."

When he heard that language directed at her, Slocum leaned in as if to grab the rider, but stopped himself before touching him. He waited to see what would happen next.

Perhaps Margaret saw what was transpiring behind the rider, because she relaxed a bit as she said, "It's written on my ledger, clear as day. I'm running a business, not trying to hide anything."

"Just tell me, damn it."

She crossed her arms and stood her ground. "I'm tired of being shoved around by the likes of you. Just because you're in good with Mr. Dawson, you and the rest of your ilk think you can do as you please. We've survived one mad dog tyrant in this town and we'll survive another."

"I don't even know what the hell you're going on about," the rider snarled as he tromped inside. "What I do know is that you'll be sorry the moment I—"

He made it all of three steps before Slocum rushed up behind him, grabbed him by the collar, and hauled him straight back outside. Margaret remained still. A satisfied little smirk crept onto her face.

But Slocum wasn't about to stay in that hotel long enough to see it. He'd caught the rider off his guard and pressed his advantage as far as he could by dragging the man outside on his heels. The rider didn't even get a chance to struggle until he was being forced to the edge of the hotel's porch and shoved off its side. He yelped when his flailing legs had nothing beneath them, but the sound was cut short when his body landed on the ground and most of the wind was driven from his lungs.

Standing over the rider like impending doom, Slocum growled, "Who were you looking for?"

The rider was having a hard time sucking in a breath and his hands slapped frantically at his holster without having the necessary coordination to draw the gun he wore.

Slocum knocked the rider flat onto his back with a short kick and then dropped his other boot squarely down on the man's wrist, pinning it in place so that hand couldn't get any closer to his pistol. "You're so ready to talk tough to a lady, why don't you do the same to me right now?"

"I'll do more than talk!" the rider swore.

"Go on, then. Make your move."

All Slocum had to do to keep the rider in place was stare directly into his eyes. Pretty soon, the other man lost the head of steam he'd built up thus far. Now that the rider had calmed down somewhat, Slocum asked, "Who were you looking for?"

"Some fella new in town."

"What's his name?"

"Slocum," the rider said as he squinted in the darkness at the man directly in front of him. "Somethin' tells me you know who that is."

"Who wants to find him so badly?"

"Mr. Dawson."

"Who's that?" Slocum asked.

The rider spat out part of a laugh as he settled in to become a bit too comfortable. "You wanna meet him? Just go on into that there hotel and march up to the third floor. He owns the whole damn thing. In fact, I'll make the introductions myself. I'd love to see the look on your face when you're taken apart and tossed out like so much tr—"

Slocum ended the conversation with a punch that was more like a hammer driving the rider's head into the ground. He leaned down to put all of his weight behind the blow as his knuckles pounded against the other man's nose. Cartilage was mashed against bone and the back of the rider's head knocked against the ground, putting the man's lights out completely.

The first thing Slocum did was drag the body into the thick shadows alongside the hotel. He then stooped down to check on the extent of the damage he'd done. The rider wasn't going to be getting up anytime soon, but he wasn't going to die either. Slocum shook the pain from his hand and hurried back to the stable.

10

"What happened?" Anna asked in a hushed whisper.

Slocum had returned to the stable, finding her clutching the edge of the door as if it was the only thing keeping her upright. "How much could you see from here?" he asked.

"I saw you grab that man and beat him mercilessly."

"It wasn't as bad as all that." He shook his hand once more as a jolt of pain lanced through his knuckles. A good amount of blood covered his hand, but he couldn't rightly say how much of it was his and how much had spilled from the rider's face. "All right," he admitted, "perhaps it did seem rather bad from where you stood. There was a reason for what I did, though."

"I'd like to hear it," Anna said as she stood with both hands propped upon her hips.

"I tossed him around like that so he couldn't get his bearings," he explained. "When I spoke to him, his head was spinning so much that he wouldn't be able to see much of anything in the dark."

"And the beating?"

"That was to make tonight even hazier when he tries to

think back on it. If the subject comes up again later, which I'm pretty certain it will, he'll be hard-pressed to say if it truly was me who knocked him out."

She shook her head and looked toward the quiet figure lying sprawled on the ground. "I know you better than that, John. You're not so foolish to think that makes much sense."

Slocum had walked all the way to the rear of the stable and found a narrow back door. Easing it open, he checked outside to find only a cool, rustling breeze waiting for him. "All right, then. He was cussing at that nice woman working the front desk and threatening her. If the asshole rides up and feels free to speak like that to someone, I'm guessing he deserved to get knocked onto his back. How's that for an explanation?"

She strode forward and took his bloody hand in both of hers. "At least it's honest," she said with a weary smile. "Do you intend on going back into that hotel?"

"Not tonight. Not until I can get a better grip on what's going on around here. Have you been in town the whole time since I left?"

"Yes."

"Then maybe you can help."

"I can tell you plenty," she said. "Just not in the dark like this. It's making me nervous."

"Me, too."

She led him out through the back door. "Come on," Anna said. "Your horse will be fine right here."

"You sure about that?"

"Even if that man you hit knows what horse you rode in on, I doubt he'll be looking to take out any hard feelings on it instead of you." Turning to look at him over one shoulder, she added, "I don't live far from here. Perhaps you remember?"

Slocum felt bad for not remembering. Instead of saying as much, he nodded and allowed himself to be dragged down an alley and across one street. The town was mostly dark apart from a few more torches scattered along the way. As he moved through Mescaline, plenty of memories rushed back into Slocum's head. Most were just fleeting glances that drifted through his mind like dreams. When he focused on the woman who had a hold of him, he remembered a good deal more.

One of the things he liked most about Anna was the way she maintained a sunny disposition no matter how dark the night became. She didn't exactly skip away from the Three Star Hotel, but she managed to glance back and smile at him with genuine warmth. Every so often, she squeezed his hand. When they got back to her little house a couple streets away, Slocum was treated to the lingering smells of freshly baked bread and candle wax. Those scents, while not uncommon, brought back more memories than anything else so far.

By the time they were inside her home and the door was shut behind him, Slocum felt as if he'd never left. Anna let go of his hand and promptly disappeared into the kitchen. "Sit down anywhere you like," she called out from the other room. "I'm getting something for that hand."

"It's all right," he replied. "Maybe just something to clean it off a bit."

Anna emerged from the kitchen and stepped into the warm light provided by the candles burning in their holders from a pair of small tables located near the door and on the opposite side of the sitting room. Most of the time, Slocum might feel confined in such close quarters. Being there with her, on the other hand, felt as if the two of them had been shut away from the rest of the world. It wasn't a bad feeling.

It was lighter in the kitchen, and as she walked toward him carrying a wet cloth, her long brown hair and trim body were outlined in the soothing glow from the other room. "Let me see that hand," she said.

Slocum stood in front of a rocker and held up his cut hand without offering it to her. "It's fine. Just hand over that cloth and I'll see to it."

"No," she insisted. When she grabbed his hand, there was no question that she would have her way. Rather than fight her on the matter, Slocum allowed her to fuss over him a bit. "There, now," she whispered. "Is that so bad?"

"Not bad at all."

"The way you carry on, you'd swear I was trying to saw your arm off. Of course, if memory serves me correct, you never were the sort to sit still long enough to be tended to."

"What are you talking about?" Slocum asked.

Anna dabbed at his hand with the cloth, cleaning away the thicker patches of blood and then gently pressing it against the spots on his knuckles where the skin had been torn asunder. "Maybe your memory isn't so good after all. When you started butting heads with Jeremiah Hartley, you were cut up, shot, stabbed . . ."

"I think you're exaggerating. It wasn't all that bad." When she didn't answer right away, he added, "Was it?"

"I had to patch you up a few times."

"Clean me up maybe," he admitted, "but that's only because I let you."

Now it was her turn to take the defensive. "You *let* me? If I was such a pest, then why on earth would you do something like that?"

She'd pulled away from him, but Slocum grabbed her wrist in a firm grip that was just tight enough to keep her from getting too far. "Because," he said gently, "I like it when you fuss over me."

The hint of anger that had flashed in her eyes disappeared as quickly as it had arrived. Anna lowered her head and took hold of his hand so she could resume cleaning it. The cloth was soaked in water and alternated between refreshing Slocum and sending sharp jabs through his cuts. He allowed her to finish her task as he watched the way her hair drifted against the side of her face and how the scant bit of light in the room played off the surface of her moist lips.

"I can get some bandages," she said.

"That might not be a great idea. After all, that would just make it clear as day I was the one who knocked that fella out."

"Then you should have thought about that before acting like such a damned bloodthirsty fool."

Her words were spoken partly in jest but rang true, and Slocum wasn't about to say otherwise. Instead, he simply stood quietly and let her work. "There," she said after a while. "All finished. Looks like it doesn't need a bandage after all."

"You're real good at that," he said while getting to his feet.

She stood as well, as if preparing to head back to the kitchen. "You've given me plenty of practice."

Taking the cloth from her, Slocum tossed it aside and placed both hands upon her hips. "I recall that you were pretty good at other things, too."

Ann responded by sliding her fingers through his hair and tossing his hat to the floor. "What do you mean, *pretty good?*"

"Guess you'll just have to remind me."

With that, Slocum kissed her. Her body was just as warm as it had been all those times when he thought back to those bloody nights during his first stay in Mescaline. At that moment, he couldn't recall why he'd been in town apart from being with her. Any unpleasantness drifted away to be forgotten as he scooped her up into his arms and carried her to the little bedroom near the back of the house.

"Aren't you a bit nervous?" she whispered.

"About what?"

"About that man knowing you're the one who hit him."

"I won't have to worry about that," Slocum replied, "until the morning."

"What about those questions you wanted to ask me?"

Slocum set her down onto a small, creaky bed. Her head was propped upon a short stack of pillows and her limbs draped like the dress that hung off her slender shoulders. "I can't think of any questions right now," he said. "Maybe I'll come up with a few later."

After that, he let his actions speak for him. Slocum peeled off her dress and crawled on top of her so he could run his hands up and down the length of her body while kissing her urgently upon her neck and chest. Anna's breasts were small and supple, capped by dark little nipples that stood erect with the slightest bit of coaxing from his fingers. She sighed and squirmed on the bed, anxious to be out from beneath him so she could start to undress him as well.

He stood up and allowed her to unbuckle his belt and pull off his shirt. The longer he waited for her to complete her task, the tenser his body became. Anna ran her hands flat against his chest and stomach, hesitating before reaching between his legs. She looked up at him and then eased his pants down, drawing an excited breath when she saw his hard cock exposed before her.

She stood in front of him, touching him gently at first, watching his face as if Slocum might have any possible objection to the way she fondled and cupped him. Wrapping one hand around his shaft, she started to stroke and smiled as he became even harder. She gasped in surprise when he suddenly lifted her up and held her in place with both hands gripping her tight little backside. Anna was quick to wrap her arms and legs around him, kissing him with growing passion as her tongue slipped into his mouth.

Her hot breath flowed against Slocum's lips, and as she writhed against him, he could feel the wetness of her pussy grinding against his rigid member. Anna rubbed her breasts on his chest, causing her to purr like a kitten as she savored the feel of her tender nipples scraping against his coarse skin. When he shifted her just enough for him to position the tip of his penis between her legs, Anna started to moan in expectation of what was to come.

With a bit more squirming and a gentle thrust, Slocum was able to penetrate her. Anna drew a deep breath and leaned her head back while he slid into her. At first, she allowed him to pump his hips between her legs, but soon she was grinding in time to his rhythm. Her grip around the back of his neck tightened and she placed her mouth against his ear so Slocum could hear her as she moaned softly when he drove deeper inside her.

"Yes," she said. "Even better than . . . better than I remember."

Slocum could have held her there all night long, but decided to set her down onto the edge of the bed. As soon as she felt the soft blankets beneath her, Anna released him and leaned back with both arms propped behind her. Fixing her eyes intently upon him, she spread her legs wide and licked her lips. Anna's slick pussy beckoned to him and it wasn't long before Slocum answered that call. He positioned himself in front of her, guided his cock into the little patch of soft hair between her thighs, and drove all the way into her warm, moist embrace.

There was just enough light in the little room for him to see the lines of Anna's body. Her skin was smooth and her long hair flowed over both shoulders to brush against her breasts. Slocum stepped in closer so he could pump into her even deeper. Anna let out a throaty moan and closed her eyes. She arched her back when she felt Slocum's hands cup her tits and gently massage. Placing one hand upon his, she guided him back and forth between her breasts and eventually to her mouth as she sucked on his fingers to taste the sweat that he'd removed from her flesh. Slocum's other hand moved down along her thigh before searching for the sensitive nub just above the spot where he entered her. When he found it, Anna began to tremble. He slowed his pace while tracing little circles against her clit.

Unable to support herself with her arms, Anna lay back and grabbed on to her bed. She gritted her teeth and writhed slowly as Slocum reached down to take hold of her ass in both hands. He could feel the muscles tensing beneath the smooth curve of her backside. Anna's entire body was quaking as he pounded into her again and again.

Whenever he thrust forward, he pulled her toward him. That way, his cock drove as deep as possible between her legs. Anna's climax wracked her entire body. Her eyes were shut tightly, and every breath escaped her in a low, almost animal grunt. When she became silent, Slocum knew she was close to her peak. He slid almost all the way out of her, paused for a few moments, and then impaled her while gripping her buttocks and holding her an inch or two off the bed.

"Oh God!" she wailed. "Yes!"

Hearing her cry out and feeling the way her pussy cinched in around him were more than enough to bring Slocum to a similar state. He pumped between her legs with mounting urgency as a rush of pleasure built up inside him. Somewhere along the line, Anna placed her legs upon his shoulders so Slocum could grab them and open them as wide as he wanted. From his angle he could pump in and out of her in powerful strokes until he exploded inside her.

Slocum grabbed her tightly and hung on until the flood of sensations passed. Once they did, he found he barely had enough strength in his legs to remain standing.

"Now," Anna said as he lay down beside her. "About those questions."

"Wh-What questions?"

11

A few hours later, after Slocum and Anna had had one more tussle in bed and some time to recover from it, he sat at the little round table in her dining room while she put together something to eat in the kitchen. "So," she said from the other room, "you're pretty easy to distract. I suppose those other things you wanted to talk about weren't so important."

"I wish that was the case," he replied. "Some other matters are just more important."

She emerged from the kitchen carrying a cup of water and a plate with a few slices of bread and some hunks of cheese on it. Even in the dim light of the single candle in the dining room, her smile was easy to see. "Important shouldn't be confused with urgent," she said. "Although one seems very much like the other when certain moods strike."

Slocum waited for her to come back with her own cup of water so he could look her in the eyes and say, "I know what I mean and *important* was the word I was after."

Sitting down across from him, Anna sipped her water and then patted his hand. "You don't have to stay here with me, John."

"Where else would I want to go?"

"Where there's a fight waiting. That's the sort of man you are."

Recoiling a bit, he said, "I'm not quite sure if I should be offended by that or not."

Rather than try to reclaim the hand that Slocum had reeled in, Anna picked up her cup and took a drink. Shrugging, she said, "It's nothing to be ashamed of. And I don't see why you'd be surprised to hear me say it."

"Guess I didn't know you thought of me like that."

"Like what? A fighter? That's what you are. The last time you were in Mescaline, you met Jeremiah Hartley and couldn't resist fighting him."

"It's not like I couldn't resist . . ."

"Really?" she asked through an amused grin. "You could have just ridden away. Lord knows plenty of other folks did."

"Would you have preferred I did?"

"Of course not. We needed a fighter. I happen to like fighters. I like to think of myself as one, just so long as it's the right sort of fight. Don't get your nose all bent out of shape just because of the words I'm using. I never called you a wild dog or bloodthirsty killer."

Slocum weighed what she said and quickly realized Anna was right. He truly was just getting his feathers ruffled because of how he'd taken one word and twisted it into something offensive. "All right," he sighed, deciding to let one matter drop so he could move on to another. "There is a fight out there waiting and normally I don't mind wading into a good scrap for the right reasons. That being said, there's plenty of good reasons for me to stay with you."

"Like?"

"Like . . . I rented a room directly below a hornet's nest and I don't particularly care to have my door kicked in while I'm asleep."

She tore off a piece of bread and stuck it into her mouth.

"So you'd rather I get *my* door kicked in? I take back what I said about you being chivalrous."

"You never said I was chivalrous."

Pausing with her cup raised partway to her lips, she shrugged and said, "I may have been thinking it at one point or another, but that's passed."

Slocum tore off some bread as well. Although it wasn't warm and was starting to get a bit crusty, it still tasted good and went down nice and easy with a sip of water. "I'd never do anything to put you in danger. We both know that. Tonight was fine because I bought us a little time. Once I'm introduced to this Mr. Dawson fellow, I suppose I'll probably go back to the Three Star."

"Why would you do that?"

"Because it's never a bad idea to keep your enemies within arm's reach. Besides, I'm not even certain he is an enemy after all. He could just have some loudmouthed assholes on his payroll."

"No," Anna snapped. "What I meant was why would you want to be introduced to Mr. Dawson? I can tell you right now that would only spell out a heap of trouble for you."

"From what I've heard, Mr. Dawson has put out some sort of bounty for me," Slocum said as he ripped into the bread as if he were stripping flesh from bone. "I don't particularly care for that. Even so, there's a chance it could just be one big misunderstanding."

"It isn't."

After chewing his bread and taking a drink, Slocum asked, "Are you going to tell me who this Dawson fella is or do I have to start guessing?"

"Isn't it clear enough already? He's the one that stepped into the space left by Jeremiah Hartley."

"Is he Jeremiah's kin?" Slocum asked.

Anna allowed her head to droop forward. Although subtle, the motion was as somber as a beautiful flower wilting from lack of water. "He's not related to Jeremiah Hartley," she told him. "At least, he's never made that known. All I can tell you for certain is that, in some ways, he's worse than Hartley ever was."

"How so?"

"Hartley may have been a mad dog, but at least a person knows what to expect with a mad dog. Until it can be put down, you stay out of its way. Blood was spilled and this town was turned into a battlefield, but that was when things boiled over. With Dawson, things haven't even gotten to a boil yet."

"Why don't you start from the beginning," Slocum said. "Who is this man?"

She pulled in a deep breath to steel herself. Maintaining her hold upon her cup, Anna kept both hands wrapped around it while swirling the remaining water around as she spoke. "After you left, Jeremiah Hartley was gone and Mescaline was able to pick itself up and dust itself off. Things became quiet. We elected a new sheriff since the last one . . . well . . . you know what Hartley did to the last one."

Slocum thought back to the bloody mess that had once been a sheriff, which had been dumped onto Main Street. As near as he could tell, Mescaline's lawman had been drawn and quartered by Hartley and three of his boys. Parts of the sheriff were scattered about town and the head was hung from a post as an example of what anyone else could expect if they crossed him or his gang. It wasn't long after that when Slocum took the offensive and wiped out Jeremiah Hartley's gang over the course of a few days.

"Yeah," he said as those haunting memories flashed through his mind. "I remember."

"Abel Dawson rode into town a few months later," she continued. "He got in good with the new sheriff. Even took a job as a deputy so he could get to know folks around here and they could get to know him. Funny thing is, he's a friendly enough sort. Easy to like. Always wanted to help.

Then one day, he announces he wants to throw his hat into the ring for mayor."

Slocum sifted through some more thoughts before admitting, "I didn't know Mescaline had a mayor."

"We don't. Not really. There's Old Man Garrett, who sits on a few committees to plan town business, but we never had need of an official mayor. We tended to our matters well enough, but that didn't seem good enough for Dawson. He pled his case to every council we have, telling us how Mescaline is growing and every town worth its salt needs to be run properly, and to do that, a town needs a proper mayor."

"So he was elected?"

She shook her head solemnly. "He tried to put together an election. He even tried to convince Old Man Garrett to put one together. But the men sitting on those committees were set in their ways and couldn't be convinced that anything different needed to be done. Mescaline is still small and we were all nervous about one man being at the head of everything. Jeremiah Hartley never declared himself the mayor, but folks around here still remembered how it was when he was around and we liked having our town back to run as we saw fit."

"Makes sense," Slocum said.

"We thought so. We even took a vote to see if we should change the way we do things around here."

"A vote to see if you wanted to hold an election? That's kind of funny."

The smile that started to appear on her face was short-lived. "Dawson acted surprised when he was told we were going to entertain his notion about a mayor one final time. He came to the town hall meeting, all dressed in his Sunday best, as if he'd already won the chair at the head of the table. When Old Man Garrett called the meeting to order, there was something strange about him. He seemed . . . frightened. And I've never known the old man to be frightened by anything. When the motion wasn't passed . . . Garrett looked positively terrified."

"What did Dawson do?"

"Nothing. He stood up, turned his back on the whole room, and walked away. A few days later Old Man Garrett's grandson, Randy Garrett, went missing. He went for a ride and didn't come back. Folks started to worry and a search party was formed. They went out to look for him." She paused to take a few silent moments and Slocum didn't try to spur her on. He just sat there and waited patiently until she said, "Nobody found a trace of him for days. Then one of the men came back with bad news. They found Randy dead in the middle of the desert. His head was cracked open by a rock. His back was broke. Both legs busted."

"Jesus."

"Best guess was that he'd been thrown from his horse and took a nasty fall, but the old man wouldn't have any of it. Randy was the apple of his eye. The poor soul was only sixteen years old. A fine young man who was always sweet to everyone he saw. Everyone in town cried at that young man's funeral. Even Abel Dawson."

When Anna spoke that man's name, it was as if she were uttering a profanity so foul that she feared retribution just for allowing it to pass her lips. Hers was a face that wasn't made to reflect such an emotion, but there it was. Even in the flickering shadows cast by the candle closest to her, Slocum could see it plain as day. "Sounds like a terrible accident," he said, feeling guilty for prodding her to return to such a grisly subject.

"It wasn't an accident," she whispered. "Poor Randy was busted up so badly, even the undertaker couldn't hardly stand to look at him. Old Man Garrett wasn't convinced neither. Not even for a second. He started talking to some of the committee members, telling them how he was threatened by Dawson to make sure he was given the mayor's office. When he refused to cooperate, his life was threatened again. When the old man said he was going to expose

Dawson for the snake he truly was, the old man's family was threatened."

Even if Slocum already knew where the conversation was headed, he still felt a knot tighten in his gut when those words were spoken. Anyone who'd threaten someone's family was the worst kind of devil. No matter how many times he'd seen it happen, the calluses on Slocum's soul weren't nearly thick enough to keep him from feeling the hot sting of rage when he saw it again. He hoped he would never stop feeling it. If a man became that numb, he was dangerously close to not having a soul at all.

As Slocum tightened his grip around his water cup, Anna said, "Some men went out to have a look at the spot where Randy was found. Trackers. There was even a bounty hunter that was passing through at the time and the old man paid him to have a look as well. They all said there wasn't a chance that Randy was hurt so badly in a fall. They said . . . they said they would have found more blood." She winced as she thought back to such a gruesome time, but forced herself to soldier on. "They said there weren't even enough sharp rocks or slopes to give him the kind of wounds he had."

"He could have been trampled by his horse," Slocum offered.

"He wasn't. His horse was found less than a quarter mile from where Randy was killed. There wasn't a hint of blood to be found on his shoes, hooves, or coat. Once Randy was found, the old man devoted every waking moment to figuring out what had happened. He told several folks how he was threatened and apparently he wasn't the only one. Some others were also threatened to convince them to get another mayoral election started."

"Are you sure about what was said behind closed doors?" Slocum asked. "Rumors can do more damage than a gun if they get far enough out of hand."

"I was at those committee meetings," she told him.

"When you and Jeremiah Hartley were fighting over this town, I saw more than I would have liked and I'd be damned if I was going to stand aside and let anything like that happen again. When I heard the first word that Abel Dawson might be trying to force himself where he wasn't wanted, I sat in on every committee meeting and made sure to be present whenever there were more than two men in town hall. I heard plenty, John. Believe that."

"I believe it. Go on."

"Once Old Man Garrett heard what the trackers and bounty hunter had to say, he just about lost his mind. He called Dawson out right in front of the house where Dawson was staying at the time. Not only Dawson, but two other men came out to answer him."

"Who were the other two?" Slocum asked.

"I never saw them before, but they were armed. Garrett made his accusations and Dawson listened. I wasn't there when this happened, but word has it that Dawson was smiling while Garrett had tears streaming down his face as he talked about his grandson. Dawson said the old man was delusional and walked back into his house. That night . . . that night Garrett's wife and son were killed. Both had their throats slit. The town was appalled, and Dawson . . . he had the nerve to say that a mother and son had gotten into a fight and killed each other in the scuffle."

"What did Garrett have to say to that?"

"Nothing. Not a word."

When he'd been in Mescaline before, Slocum had met Old Man Garrett on more than a few occasions. The moniker may have sounded disrespectful, but it was more commonly used than his rightful name. Garrett was a kindhearted man who quickly befriended just about anyone he met. The old man had plenty of sand and was one of the first to help Slocum win the fight against Jeremiah Hartley. It was damn near inconceivable that the old man would have stood by and said nothing at a time like the one Anna was describing.

"An election was held," she said in a dull monotone. "Dawson was elected mayor even though nobody really knew what that entailed. Apart from those on the committees, nobody even knew the matter was going to be brought up again until the day before ballots were cast. Even though everyone I've asked say they voted against the proposition, it was passed and the office was created. Dawson strode into it like a proud poppa and set up his home and offices on the third floor of the Three Star Hotel. Two days after that, Old Man Garrett marched in to have a word with him."

"That sounds more like the man I knew," Slocum said. "How many others did he bring with him?"

"None."

"Not even someone to watch his back?"

"No," she said quietly. "Witnesses saw him go in, but nobody saw him leave. There were a few guesses . . . involving bundles that were taken out and dumped in the desert . . . but nobody knows for certain. All I can tell you, John, is that whenever someone asked around about what happened to the old man, they became real quiet on the subject shortly after. I asked some of the committee members what they thought might have happened. They were two men I thought I could trust. The next day, one of Dawson's men walks into the restaurant where I worked and told me they'd . . . well . . . let's just say he had nothing but ugly words."

"Tell me what they said."

"No. I . . ."

Slocum reached out to place his hand on top of hers. Squeezing gently but insistently, he said, "I want to know what he said."

"Don't make me say it."

"He threatened your life?"

Even in the scant amount of light in the room, Slocum could tell that she paled when she replied, "He didn't threaten my life . . . but he did threaten to hurt me. Said he would . . . do things to me. I . . . it—"

"Never mind," Slocum interrupted. "I understand. It was just the one? Would you be able to point him out to me?"

"It's not that simple, John. It's not like when all we had to worry about was a crazy man with a gun. That was bad enough, but Dawson is something different."

"He may be a different kind of animal, but he still needs to be brought down a couple of pegs. For just about any animal, that job is done in much the same way."

Soon, she was the one taking his hand and squeezing urgently. "When someone stands up to Dawson, they're not just threatened. Things happen. Terrible things. The kind of things that make you wish he was just firing shots at you. And he doesn't just stop at one person. He goes after folks you know and he doesn't stop until he's gotten what he wants."

The questions Slocum was about to ask were similar to the ones he'd asked the last time he'd been in Mescaline. What about the law? What about confronting this man? What about letting him know he wasn't feared and telling him he should leave town before he was tossed out on his ear? Slocum had asked those very same things where Jeremiah Hartley was concerned, and the fact that the questions needed to be asked again about another threat to the same people put a bad taste in his mouth.

"I can tell what you're thinking," she said. "I can see the disgust on your face. You think we're all cowards."

"No," Slocum said. "That's not what I was thinking."

"Don't you think we've all thought the same thing? After what happened with Jeremiah Hartley, there have been plenty of men who stepped up to make certain it wouldn't happen again."

"And what happened to them?" Slocum asked.

"Some disappeared. Some are on Dawson's payroll now. Some are still in mourning for the loved ones that were either hurt or killed under strange circumstances. Some had houses or businesses that were burned to the ground. Some of them were burned to death inside them."

Pulling his hand from her grasp, Slocum said, "It doesn't matter how they go about it, men like Hartley and Dawson are the same. They spill blood to get what they want because they think they can get away with it. And they'll keep spilling blood until someone shows them they *can't* get away with it anymore. I've seen more men like that than I can count."

She shook her head vehemently. "You couldn't have seen anyone else like Abel Dawson. If you have, then I pity you because he's the closest thing to a devil any man can be and I've looked into the eyes of Jeremiah Hartley while he was gunning down men in the street right outside my house."

"He's a man, Anna. Just a power-hungry, bloodthirsty, back-stabbing, lying man who needs to surround himself with hired guns to get what he wants." Suddenly fed up with arguing what seemed like an obvious point, Slocum pounded the table and declared, "He's no devil!"

When Slocum grew angry, Anna became calmer. "That's not what I'm trying to say. I realize he's a man. I see that he's surrounding himself with gunmen. What I'm telling you is that you can't just walk up to Abel Dawson like he was some ordinary killer. He's more than that."

"Tell me what he is, then."

"He's someone that will not just hurt you, but will wait until he knows what you hold dear and then hurt that. He'll come in the middle of the night and do unspeakable things to anything or anyone you cherish before doing the same to you. He's not interested in a fight. He only cares about winning whatever prize he's set his sights on."

"What prize is that?" Slocum asked.

"I don't know, John. I just want to stay out of his way until I get a chance to be free of this godforsaken town."

"Then I guess it's up to me to find out what he's after."

12

That night, Slocum barely slept. His thoughts were filled with words that had been spoken, memories of all kinds, and plans for all the different ways he could approach Abel Dawson. Of course, his first option was not to approach him at all. That was always a choice, but rarely a good one. Once a man started running from a fight, he never stopped running. In Slocum's case, he knew he wouldn't be able to look at himself in a mirror if he knew he'd turned tail and left town after what he'd heard.

For one thing, whoever Dawson was or whatever he wanted, he'd put a price on Slocum's head. That was something Slocum simply could not abide. Whether Dawson was Jeremiah Hartley's kin or not, the legacy of one most certainly influenced the actions of the other.

Another thing that troubled him was how an entire town could allow a man like that to seize control again. No matter how much he tried to sympathize, part of Slocum couldn't help but feel angry that so many good people could just roll over like a bunch of whipped dogs when another armed man came along and snapped his fingers. There was obviously more to it than that, but the fact remained that the people who'd survived one such ordeal should have learned enough to make certain it didn't happen again.

All of those things and plenty more were boiling inside Slocum's head as he got up and went into Anna's kitchen after a fitful night's rest. She joined him soon after and prepared a simple breakfast of oatmeal and coffee without more than a handful of words passing between them.

Outside, the sun was making itself known only by coloring the sky a light, hazy purple. Cold, crisp air seeped into the house from all sides like icy fingers encircling them within the desert's chilling grip. Slocum ate the food that was placed in front of him, got dressed, buckled his gun belt around his waist, and placed his hat upon his head. He was reaching for the handle of the front door when Anna stopped him with two little words.

"Don't go."

"Gunmen were sent to collect my scalp. I can't let a thing like that stand."

"Why not? Surely this isn't the first time someone's threatened you like that."

"No," Slocum replied. "It isn't. If I let it go unanswered, though, it may be the last."

Standing behind him, she asked, "Why? Are you afraid of what people say about you when you're not there to defend yourself? There's worse things than bad talk dirtying your name."

"This man Dawson didn't just appear at the edge of the desert and ride into Mescaline," Slocum said as he wheeled around to find Anna standing with her arms crossed and a stern expression etched into her face. "If his offer makes it out of this town, there'll be men in other towns looking to collect. And if the offer stands without someone answering for it, more like it will spring up. There are plenty of men who would pay to have my head upon their platter. I've got to make it known what a bad idea that is."

She approached him, looking as though she would continue to address him in a severe manner. As soon as she unfolded her arms and wrapped them around him, she took on a much softer tone. "You've already saved this town once, John. You don't have to risk your life doing it again."

"You're getting ahead of yourself," he said while embracing her. "I came to Mescaline to conduct some business and that's what I intend on doing."

"You'll steer clear of Abel Dawson?"

"I won't seek out a fight."

"Just promise me you'll steer clear of him."

"I can't do that," he said. "From what you told me, he's got this town wrapped around his finger. Besides, if the fella that was threatening the woman at the Three Star is awake and talking, he'll let them know something happened. He was already looking for me, so I guess they'll find me sooner or later."

"I forgot about him," she sighed. Holding him at arm's length, Anna looked up at Slocum and said, "You don't have to go back to the Three Star."

"That's where my gear is. I'm not about to abandon it."

"Damn it, John! You're taking this too lightly!"

Slocum eased some of her worries with a kiss. They'd shared plenty of them since he'd arrived, but this one was more like a cool breeze than the fiery passion from the previous night. "I'm not taking this lightly," he said in a voice that was just loud enough for her to hear. "Trust me, I'm not about to stroll in anywhere unless I've got something up my sleeve."

After allowing him to slip from her grasp, Anna asked, "Do you truly have something up your sleeve this time?"

"Always. But I won't be able to do this on my own."

"If there's anything I can do to help . . ."

"What I need," Slocum replied, "is very important and it seems perfectly suited to your particular talents."

He spoke to her for another couple of minutes. Although she was intrigued by his proposition, she was also more than a little leery. "Are you sure this can work?" she asked when he was done spelling everything out for her.

"It's got to."

Whenever Slocum had thought back to Mescaline in the days following his run-in with Jeremiah Hartley, he didn't think of it as a particularly quiet or rowdy town. Of course, that was when he thought of the town itself and not the chaos brought by the mad dog outlaw who'd tried keeping the place under his boot. Mescaline was still fairly small, which meant it would be quiet after sundown. What Slocum experienced as he made his way back to the Three Star that morning, however, was more than just quiet.

It was silence more suited for a grave.

The sun had crested the eastern horizon, spreading brighter colors across the sky like so much spilled paint. It was Slocum's experience that town folk tended to sleep later than ranch hands or cowboys, simply because their professions made different demands of them. Even so, there were plenty of reasons for folks in town to greet the sunrise every morning that didn't involve tending animals, planting crops, or preparing for a long day's ride.

Perhaps what struck Slocum the most was the fact that he could see signs of life all around him. Smoke rose from chimneys. Curtains rustled in windows. He even got a few fleeting glimpses of people moving in doorways. For some reason, though, none of those people seemed interested in poking their noses outside. Then, as if to prove him wrong, a single horse pulled a cart around the corner directly in front of him. The cart was driven by a man who sat with the reins in his hands, his back hunched over, and a floppy, wide-brimmed hat angled forward to cover most of his face. A slack-jawed mouth hung partly open as it gnawed on a thick piece of hay.

"Morning," Slocum said cheerily.

The cart driver used one dirty hand to push his hat up

enough for him to gander at something other than the backside of the animal in front of him. After taking Slocum's stock in a slow down-and-up glance, he grunted and gave his reins a flick. The horse picked up its pace, carrying the cart a little faster down the street.

Slocum guessed the driver of that cart wouldn't have provided much in the way of conversation, but he didn't have anything for comparison. He didn't cross anyone else's path before arriving at the Three Star. When he opened the door to the hotel, he was greeted with a whole different scene entirely.

There was a different woman tending the front desk. She was a short lady in her fifties with dark hair tied into a bun and a wide smile that was almost as bright as the rising sun. She was talking to a man who leaned against the desk on an elbow as if he'd bellied up to a bar. Voices filled the hotel as conversations, laughter, and plenty more drifted through the air along with the scents of frying bacon, eggs, and potatoes. Upon seeing him enter, the woman behind the counter brightened even more.

"Do my eyes deceive me?" she asked. "Is that John Slocum?"

He strode forward and put on a smile to match hers. "Your eyes do not deceive you, ma'am."

"I saw the name on my register and thought it was someone coming around trying to get a few free drinks."

"Does that happen often?"

"You'd be surprised what some unethical types will do for free drinks or otherwise favorable treatment," she said. "What can I do for you?"

"First of all, I'd like some breakfast."

"Go right in, take any seat you like. Margaret is in the kitchen right now and she said she'll whip up some biscuits and gravy as soon as you're ready for them."

"Just as long as you bring them to me yourself," Slocum replied with a grin.

The woman's cheeks flushed a bit, but she quickly agreed.

Slocum went into the dining room and had to look around for a table that wasn't already being used. Eventually, he found one in a corner at the back of the room close to the door leading to the kitchen. Since the table allowed him to put his back to a wall and the rest of the room directly in front of him, it was perfectly suited to his needs.

"I guess this is where everyone went," he said to himself as he took a seat and removed his hat. By the time he'd placed his hat on the back of the chair beside him, Slocum could see the top of the short woman's head moving through the crowd like a fish navigating a messy coral reef.

She exchanged quick pleasantries with several of the patrons and tossed him an even quicker nod as she charged into the kitchen. In no time at all, she came out again carrying a steaming cup resting in a white saucer. Somehow she managed to dodge a few servers and several meandering customers without spilling a drop from the cup which she placed in front on him on the table.

"There you go," she said. "Freshly brewed. The rest is on its way."

Slocum could smell the coffee right away. He picked up the cup and moved it beneath his nose to take an even deeper breath. "I'm surprised there's any left," he said. "You're awfully busy this morning."

"It's busy every morning."

"Any particular reason for that?" he asked as he shifted his eyes to study her.

Even though he couldn't recall the woman's name, Slocum knew he'd seen her before. The lines on her face, while put there by age, didn't do a thing to dim the light that shone inside her. She was a radiant woman, brimming with a good nature and kind soul. All those things made Slocum feel even worse for not being able to think of her name.

In response to the question that had been posed to her, she shrugged. "We serve a good breakfast. The Three Star has some of the finest cooks in Nevada in its employ. That's mostly because of our distinguished guest on the third floor, but he's probably the other reason so many folks are here."

"You mean Mr. Dawson?"

"That's right. So you've heard of him?"

"Hard not to hear of a man like that," Slocum replied.

For the first time since he'd walked into the hotel, Slocum saw the cordial expression on her face dim. The woman, not much taller than him while he was seated, quickly regained her previous brightness as she said, "Men like him aren't difficult to find. All you have to do is look under a rock in damp places."

"He seems to be important."

"Here in Mescaline, he is. But this is a small town in a small desert on the face of a very large world. In the scheme of things, Dawson isn't much more than a bump on a forgotten log. Now is there anything else I can get for you?"

"Aren't you going to ask me why I'm here?" Slocum said.

"I figured you'd tell me," she replied. "If I listen long enough, folks tend to tell me everything there is about themselves. After all, that's usually their favorite subject."

"It pains me to admit this, but I don't recall your name."

Her smile returned in all its glory. "That's not surprising," she said. "Especially considering how busy you were during your last visit. Some know me as Lacy."

Slocum furrowed his brow. "That doesn't sound familiar. Why do they call you that?"

"Because they weren't listening well enough to have heard my name is actually Lucy."

"Too busy talking about their favorite subject, huh?"

She tapped her temple and winked at him.

"Well, your real name sounds more familiar," Slocum said. "I think that's the one I'll use."

"Glad to hear it."

When Lucy started to move away from the table to check on his breakfast, he took hold of her arm in a grip that was just firm enough to keep her from getting far. "Did you hear about what happened the other night?"

"You mean about you getting to town or about one of Dawson's men being dragged out into the night and knocked into a stupor?" Looking at him as if she knew more than anyone else in that entire room, she said, "Yes. I did hear. You wouldn't have had something to do with any of that, would you?"

"I most certainly did! I got to town on my own steam. Rode all the way through that little desert you mentioned."

"What about the rest?"

"The rest," Slocum said. "Well, that's what I wanted to talk to you about."

"I should warn you, John. This may be that little inconsequential place I described earlier, but while you're here, Dawson is still at the head of the table. Most everyone who comes to court his favor will do so any way they can, even if it means feeding a good man like yourself to the wolves."

"Then I suggest you take a seat and look as if I'm not saying anything more than my thoughts on the weather."

She placed her hand upon the back of the chair Slocum offered and leaned in. "I still need to get your breakfast. Can it wait?"

"While you're back there, can you tell me if there are any of Dawson's men in the kitchen?"

"I can tell you that right now," she replied. "Any men Dawson might have are right where you can see them. He's confident enough that he doesn't feel he needs to worry about someone taking a run at him. That is, unless that someone is you."

"Does he force everyone to stay inside?"

Lucy frowned and asked, "What do you mean?"

"Because the only person I saw on the street on my way over here was one fella driving a cart and he didn't seem interested in giving so much as a how-do-you-do."

"Oh yes," she said with a weary nod. "After spending

every day in this place, it's easy to regard these conditions as normal. Our great and illustrious benefactor," she declared while sweeping an arm toward the upper floors, "has imposed a curfew meant to keep the streets clear."

"What's the reason for that?"

"He says it's to keep the amount of noise and rowdiness down to acceptable levels. Since Mescaline never was much for rowdiness, apart from those nights when you were last here, I'd say it's more likely that he just wants to keep this town under control any way he can. If he can tell us when to go about our affairs, then he has an easier time controlling everything else."

"And what happens if someone breaks the curfew?" Slocum asked.

"That person gets locked into a cell."

"They just get locked away? How can that stand?"

"It's just for a night or maybe a few hours," she explained. "Any outsider might see it as well within reason. But you see, he keeps a certain number of animals locked away in the town's jail, and if anyone breaks even the smallest ordinance, they get thrown in with them. You don't want to know who is in there, John. I don't even know their names. They're rapists, killers, the worst kind of men there are, and they make one night in that jail worse than a night in hell. Dawson uses it as a way to keep folks in line while he's still able to shrug his shoulders and claim he's simply upholding the letter of the law. Anyone speaks out against the law and . . . well . . . bad things happen."

"I've heard about that. Have any of your people spread the word about me being here?"

"Not on your life," she said quickly. "You saved the lives of just about everyone in this town. The last thing we'd want to do is set you up to be gunned down by the likes of him."

"From what I hear, that's not his style," Slocum pointed out.

"In general, you'd be right." In a low whisper, she added,

"He's afraid of you, I think. Perhaps you already know about the reward he's offered?"

"When did he post that?"

"As soon as he took certain steps against upstanding members of this community."

"I heard what he did to Old Man Garrett," Slocum said. "That's a damn shame."

"More than a shame," she said in a stern, grave tone. "It's a sin. A sin, I'm hoping, that won't go unanswered."

"I'm not in the business of sins or paying them back," Slocum said. "For that kind of work, I believe you're looking for a man wearing a starched white collar and carrying a Good Book in his hands."

She nodded slowly. "After what happened to Mr. Garrett and his family, Dawson set up shop in my hotel. That's also when he posted that reward for you. I doubt he was actually thinking he'd have to pay out. Like so much of what he does, it's simply to send a message. He's telling everyone here in town that they shouldn't expect anyone else to save them this time around. And if a savior does come, he'll be made an example of just like so many others have recently."

"How many others have there been?"

"Too many," she said. "Now let me get your breakfast."

"One last thing before you go. It's important." Then Slocum told her a few things in a hurry. Although he covered a lot of the same ground he had when talking to Anna, he had a few different things to say to Lucy before she got up, patted his shoulder, and walked to the kitchen.

When she returned, it was with a heaping plate of biscuits topped by thick gravy and a napkin wrapped around some silverware. She placed both down on his table before turning her attention to someone who needed her nearby. She left him to his meal without another word.

Slocum enjoyed his breakfast in peace. For the most part, folks in the dining room let him be. They seemed to have plenty of their own business to conduct and didn't take notice of the man who sat alone in one corner. Along with the biscuits, he was given a few strips of bacon cut in thick slices and fried until they were just shy of burned. There were also some potatoes chopped into a hash with some onions and tomatoes mixed in. He devoured the feast and washed it down with coffee that primed him for the rest of the day.

Although he could see several people drifting in and out of the dining room, the crowd never really grew any smaller. Whenever someone walked out, someone else walked in. Many of them checked the clock on the wall every couple of seconds, waiting for the hands to tell them that whatever curfew had been imposed on them had expired.

He saw one man enter who was different from the rest. While the others were wrapped up in their own business, this one was more concerned with studying each and every table in turn. When he found Slocum's, he walked straight through the crowd until he was close enough to stand in front of him with his hand resting upon the gun at his hip and say, "Mr. Dawson would like to have a word with you."

"Damn," Slocum replied as he folded his napkin and stood up. "Sure took him long enough."

13

Apart from what he'd said when he first approached Slocum's table, the man who'd singled him out didn't let another word slip as he led Slocum out of the dining room. Slocum followed him with an amicable look on his face, but did not let his hand drift too far from the .44 at his side.

"So," Slocum said as he walked through the hotel's lobby. "What should I call you?"

The other man didn't break his silence as he continued across the room toward the stairs leading to the second floor.

"Mind telling me what this is about?" Slocum asked.

"You'll find out soon enough," the other man said.

"If this is some sort of courtesy from the hotel, I'm not impressed."

"Go on upstairs."

"After you."

Rather than argue, the other man grabbed the banister and started climbing the stairs. The second floor was familiar enough and Slocum stopped there. The other man got to the second step in the next flight before turning around and glaring at him.

"Come on," he grunted. "We're going to the third floor."

"Not until you let me know what this is about."

What had caused him to pause was the number of men clustered at the top of the staircase. Slocum counted at least three waiting for him on the third-floor landing. He didn't have to wait long before one of those men came down the stairs in a rush and hunkered down so he could get a look at the second floor as quickly as possible. The face that dipped into Slocum's line of sight was lumpy, bruised, and somewhat familiar.

"That's him!" the bruised man said as he jabbed a finger at Slocum. "That's the one that jumped me!"

"You sure about that, Mikey?" the man who'd brought Slocum this far asked.

"Sure it was!"

"I don't know what you're talking about," Slocum said as he held his hands in front of him in a placating gesture. "I was just downstairs eating my breakfast when this gentleman here—"

"Don't give me that bullshit!" Mikey said as he stomped down some more of the stairs. "You bushwhacked me like a damn coward last night!"

"If I was in a brawl," Slocum said innocently, "don't you think I'd have a cut or blemish to show for it? That is, unless you're saying all of that damage was done to you without the other man getting so much as a scratch in return?"

There was a tension in the air, crackling like the warning rumbles of an approaching storm. Some of it lessened as the man on the staircase behind Slocum's guide stared daggers down at the second floor.

"It was dark," the bruised man said. "And I know I got my share of licks in."

"That's what I thought," Slocum said.

Baring his teeth while pointing furiously down at him, Mike said, "Don't get cocky, asshole! I got my eyes on you."

"Best keep your eyes on the man who got the better of

you," Slocum replied. "Seems like it wouldn't be wise to let him get the drop on you again."

"No. It sure wouldn't. That ain't gonna happen, I can guarantee that much."

Another man stepped onto the third-floor landing to stand behind Mike. Although Slocum couldn't see more than another shadow being cast from the floor above him, he could tell the man was more than just another body taking up space. All the others who had been crowding the top of the stairs moved aside like minnows clearing a path for a shark.

"You done, Mikey?" Slocum's guide asked.

Mike did his best to keep up his appearance as a man who was to be feared, but his battered face made that somewhat difficult. "I'm through," he said, "but I ain't going nowhere."

"That's where you're wrong, Mike," declared a booming voice that seemed to fill the entire third floor.

When he heard it, Mike winced and wheeled around as if something was about to be dropped from on high.

Rather than any sort of bloodcurdling threat, the voice said, "You're stepping aside to clear a path and you're doing it right now."

"Sure thing, Mr. Dawson," Mike said. And then, like a cat scampering away after its tail was smashed beneath a rocking chair, he got as far over to one side as the staircase would allow so he could go back to wherever he'd come from.

The man who'd parted the waters upstairs stomped halfway down the stairs and stopped. A large fellow in every sense of the word, he stood well over six feet and filled the staircase with a frame that was wide and bulky without being fat. He wore dark trousers and a simple white shirt beneath a gray vest decorated with a watch chain stretching across his midsection. There was no gun belt around his waist, but considering how all of the armed men around him waited with bated breath, he didn't exactly need one.

"This is the man you asked for," Slocum's guide announced.

Dawson regarded Slocum with eyes set in a rounded face. His mouth was set in something of a smile that could very easily be mistaken as friendly. "Where was he?"

"Eating breakfast downstairs."

"Did you let him finish?"

Looking back and forth between Slocum and Dawson, the guide replied, "No, sir."

"Well, that ain't no way to treat a guest!" When he talked, Dawson sounded like a man who was accustomed to speaking in proper grammar but thought it helped his cause to try and sound like the commoners around him. Since he seemed to already have a firm grip on just about everyone in his vicinity, it didn't really matter who bought into his act or who didn't.

Slocum smiled just enough to make it seem like he was one of the believers when he asked, "Would you mind if I went back and finished up?"

Standing sideways to clear a path, Dawson replied, "It's probably already cold by now. Since you're here, you might as well have a chat with me and I'll see to it your belly is filled when we're through."

"Sounds fair enough."

The man who'd brought Slocum this far stepped aside and made a sweeping gesture as if he were escorting him into a gilded carriage. Mike stayed back as well, but made sure he sneered at Slocum enough to convey his true feelings. Slocum met the bruised man's glare with a friendly nod that was almost enough to get Mike to strain once more against his leash.

When he got to the top of the stairs, Slocum was greeted by Dawson and the men accompanying him. There were less than half a dozen in all, but the third-floor hallway was narrow and the gunmen filled almost every available space. While none had their guns drawn, their hands practically itched above their weapons and their eyes betrayed a shared hope that one wrong move would be made so they could cut this meeting short in the bloodiest possible way.

"You'll have to excuse my men," Dawson said in what he must have thought was a sheepish manner. "They tend to get a little protective of their own."

"I can't imagine why," Slocum said.

Dawson dropped a hand upon Slocum's shoulder like a hammer. Not only did the gesture stop him in his tracks, but it made Slocum feel like a child looking up to a broad-shouldered giant. It wasn't often that Slocum felt that way. Even though he quickly shook it off, Slocum felt a pang of anger that it had been there at all.

"Don't take me for an idiot, John," Dawson said. "That is, if you don't mind me calling you that."

"Only my friends call me that."

"We're not friends?"

Slocum shook his head and slowly pulled his shoulder out from beneath Dawson's paw of a hand. "Not yet."

"Well then," the bigger man declared as he slapped Slocum on the shoulder, "we'll just have to see about rectifying that! Come along with me and I'll fix you a drink."

Although Slocum could have pulled away so he wasn't swept down the hallway by Dawson, it would have only created a scene and the end result probably would have been the same anyway. There were more important things than being difficult just for the sake of defying someone like him.

"Bit early for a drink, wouldn't you say?" Slocum asked.

"Depends on what the drink is." Dawson didn't walk very far. He passed only one doorway before standing beside another door and motioning for Slocum to precede him inside. The door they'd passed was propped open by a man wearing dark trousers held up by silk suspenders over a pearl gray shirt. He carried a shotgun in a loose grip so the barrels were pointed at the floor. His thumb rested upon the hammers, making it clear he was ready to unleash a whole lot of sound and fury at a moment's notice.

Meeting the shotgunner's gaze, Slocum continued toward the door where Dawson was standing and walked inside. If any of these men truly meant him harm, they would have cut loose already. Inside, the room was much larger than he'd anticipated. That was probably due to the fact that it used to be a pair of smaller rooms that had been combined after the wall between them was knocked down. The floor was covered in a thick, dark red rug decorated with golden threads. A billiard table took up a good portion of one half of the room and the other half was dominated by a desk that seemed too big to have been brought all the way up to the hotel's third floor. When Dawson stepped over to it, however, the desk seemed properly suited to him.

"Most folks enjoy coffee in the morning," he said. "I prefer tea myself. Picked it up from an old English business partner of mine. We shipped crates of the stuff from all over the world. I decided to try a cup to see what all the fuss was about and I just couldn't stomach coffee again. Care to join me?"

"Sure. It's been a while since I've had any tea."

"And you've never had tea like this here," Dawson said while pouring some into a cup. The kettle was fine white porcelain and the saucer almost disappeared within his beefy hand. Even so, he handled them expertly and even lifted his little finger a bit while placing a spoon onto the saucer. "Here you go, Mr. Slocum. I'm hoping soon I'll be able to call you John."

Slocum took the cup and brought it up to his nose. The steam rising up from the tea smelled vaguely sweet even though he hadn't seen any sugar get stirred into the brew. The tea itself was light in color. "Are you sure this has steeped enough?"

"It's white tea. Give it a taste. Not your ordinary leaves are found around here."

Slocum took a sip and was pleasantly surprised by the

minty aftertaste that was left in his throat after the rest went down. "It's good."

"Only the best. Hopefully it's good enough to give us a fresh start after one hell of a rough night."

After another sip, Slocum took a slow walk around the office, taking particular notice of the windows and the view of the street below.

"Aw hell!" Dawson said in a way that shattered his previous pretenses. "I just realized! I never properly introduced myself. You must think I've got rocks in my head. I'm Abel Dawson, the mayor of this good town. It was awfully vain of me to assume my reputation would precede me, but I must say yours has laid quite a lot of groundwork here. It's good to finally meet you."

"Yeah. Must be nice to enjoy a cup of tea with a man you want to see dead."

Dawson actually had the gall to look surprised when he heard that. He even glanced about the room as if someone would be there to explain the situation to him. Finally, he raised his eyebrows and said, "Oh! The reward notice! Of course. That must be what you're referring to."

"It sure as hell is."

Waving that off with a swatting gesture, he circled around to sit behind his desk. After another sip of tea, he set it down so he could open a drawer and remove a single piece of paper. Holding it in front of him like an actor with a script, he mused, "I reckon this was just my way of nipping any trouble in the bud."

"You mean nipping *me* in the bud," Slocum pointed out.

"Mere theatrics. For dramatic effect," he said as he tossed the paper onto the desk and turned it around so Slocum could read it properly.

It looked like most other reward notices Slocum had seen in his day. At the top was a bold-faced declaration to catch the eye stating there was a reward being offered. The rest was several lines of colorful description describing how dangerous the subject was, followed by the amount being offered for his capture. Although Slocum couldn't easily count how many such notices he'd seen before, it never sat well when he was the subject being described in such a manner.

"Don't know if I like this kind of dramatic effect," Slocum said as he shoved the paper back toward Dawson.

"But I assure you that's all it was." Leaning back caused Dawson's chair to creak beneath his weight. He reached out to flip open a wooden box and remove a cigarette, which he placed between his teeth. When he spoke from then on, it sounded more like a snarl. "After you left, things were in chaos. I'm not blaming it on you, though. While I wasn't here for the whole Jeremiah Hartley situation, I heard it was pretty damn bad and you did a hell of a job in cleaning it up. You didn't want to stay behind and look after these folks . . . again," he added quickly, "I ain't casting any blame. But someone did need to look after them. If Jeremiah Hartley proved anything, it's that these people can't exactly look after themselves."

"They did just fine before Hartley," Slocum pointed out.

"That's when this place was just a bump in the road. A road, mind you, that nobody in their right mind was interested in traveling. Now there's a railroad station not too far from here in Davis Junction and there's thieves preying on them who are on their way to catch a train to places a whole lot better than this. My point is that this country is growing and even towns like Mescaline are gonna feel the pains from all that expansion. You see what I'm saying here, John?"

"I understand about expansion," Slocum replied. "But I still don't see what that has to do with offering money for my corpse."

"These folks needed someone to look out for them, but certain members of the community weren't seeing it that way. They still had their heads stuck back in the days when the occasional meeting and a few helpful souls could keep a town running. Those days are over, better or worse, like it or not."

Slocum sipped his tea and enjoyed the refreshing flavor as it washed down his throat. He didn't let any of that satisfaction show when he said, "I still don't see how this relates to that notice."

"I offered these people a solid foundation and good leadership," Dawson said as he pounded the tip of his finger against his desk with enough force to make a solid *thump*. "They repaid me by threatening to run me out of town. Since the show you put on was still fresh in their minds, many of them talked about finding you or taking your example by picking up a gun and ending their troubles with hot lead instead of civilized talk and good ideas."

"Sometimes hot lead is what's needed."

"You're right about that," Dawson replied in a tone that was as smooth and unwavering as a dagger's blade. "Some of them took a run at me when I proposed we change things around here. They tried to kill me just like the mad dog that was put into the ground back in the bloody days."

"I heard you did some damage of your own," Slocum pointed out.

"I did what was necessary to protect myself and my interests."

"And what interests would a man like yourself have in a sleepy little town like this? Would they have anything to do with a railroad line meant to be split off from Davis Junction?"

Dawson was obviously not accustomed to being blindsided. He flinched and narrowed his eyes as if he was looking at Slocum in a whole new way. "What the hell do you know about that?"

"I didn't know anything for certain . . . not until this moment."

Without taking his eyes away from Slocum, Dawson

pointed at the armed man who'd followed them inside to stand by the door and barked, "Get out. Now."

The gunman nodded and backed out as quickly as he could. The door was shut quietly in his wake.

"Tell me what you know about the railroad," Dawson demanded.

"I know plenty, Abel. That is, if you don't mind us being on a first-name basis."

Dawson didn't give his consent, but was too wound up at the moment to protest.

Moving along now that he had the reins firmly in hand, Slocum said, "I have a lot of friends in a lot of places. Many of them owe me a lot, but there are some things a man can just piece together for himself. Assets like those are what have kept me alive for so long in this hard, changing world." Subtly tossing Dawson's words back at him was a minor indulgence, but Slocum simply couldn't help himself.

"Those notices," Dawson said as he pointed to the one on his desk, "were just to make a point. To send a message that I wasn't about to be intimidated by anyone. Not even the great John Slocum. What you did where Jeremiah Hartley was concerned was a hell of a deed. But folks here were threatening to have me gunned down like a dog in the street if I didn't step aside and let them have their way."

"And your only concern was the well-being of this town," Slocum said. "Or was it to use the town and everyone in it to put a whole lot of railroad money into your pockets? Let me guess. You just need to keep folks quiet and controlled until the railroad companies come knocking?"

"I want to be prosperous," Dawson said. "Isn't that what every man wants? I also want to forge a legacy for myself and my family. That's what caused this town to grow, my friend, and that's what keeps people coming out West when there are plenty of warm beds back East. We all want to make something of ourselves. When certain folks around here started trying to force me out, I could either have given in or fought back. When I decided to fight, I could either have done it with words or with guns. I chose words. Once they saw I wasn't afraid of you, things quieted down considerably." He put on a humorless grin and settled back into his chair. "Truth be told, I never thought you'd see any of those notices. Now that you have, I'll gladly offer my apologies."

"What about the reward?" Slocum asked.

Dawson looked at him silently for a few moments before striking a match against his desk and lighting the cigarette he'd been chomping on. "What do you mean?"

"You posted this notice," Slocum said as he picked up the paper and studied it as if he were admiring a work of art. "It's in writing. Legally, you're bound to pay up if someone brings John Slocum to you. Now some of your men may have escorted me up those stairs, but I'd say it's fairly certain I'm the one that brought myself all the way back to Mescaline and into this office without the fuss you were obviously expecting."

"Those men outside? They're just there for protection."

"From who?" Slocum asked. "A town full of shopkeepers and old folks? Remember, I spent a good amount of time here not too long ago. Unless a bunch of dangerous killers have taken residence here since the last time I visited, I don't exactly see what a man like you would need with all this firepower."

"I told you. Folks around here want to be rid of me. They don't know what's good for them."

"And you do, huh?"

Dawson sat up a little straighter and replied, "I'd like to think so."

"But what am I saying? We both know there are people apart from the ones that live here who have a bone to pick with you." Slocum let that settle in for a moment, but knew better than to think Dawson would snap at the bait he was dangling without a bit more coaxing. "You must know about the assassin in Davis Junction."

"No," Dawson said. "I don't know of any assassin."

"There was a killing there. Someone who spoke up on your behalf wound up dead for mentioning your name. The next day after he made his loyalties clear, he was found cut up in a stable. Someone tried blaming me, but I don't know what that was about. All I know is that when he was going on about you and that railroad, it was the last time anyone saw him alive. My guess is someone doesn't like you or anything any of your supporters might have to say."

"What was this man's name?"

Slocum shrugged. "Derrick . . . something or other. He worked in a stable. Wasn't my concern. I was headed back here to conduct some business of my own, so I left before I was dragged into that mess. Didn't really try to figure it out. Now that I've met you and seen what's going on here, a lot of it is making much more sense."

Although Dawson's face wasn't easy to read, Slocum didn't have to look very hard to find the telltale signs of confusion and anger. No man who was as full of himself as Dawson liked to be in the dark about anything. "This is the first I've heard of any of this," he said.

"Doesn't surprise me," Slocum replied. "It was all coming to a boil when I left. I came straight here, so I didn't bother looking into it. I wouldn't mind doing just that, however."

"You wouldn't?" Dawson asked through a suspicious scowl.

Slocum shook his head. "Of course not. There'd be one condition, though."

"What's that?"

Slocum took one last sip of tea before gently placing the cup down. "I'd have to be cut in on some of the profits."

"You mean be on my payroll?" Dawson asked with a shark-like smile.

"No," Slocum replied. "I won't be just another hired gun.

You've already got more than enough of those. I'm talking about getting a cut of the profits with this railroad deal."

Dawson still looked like a hungry predator when he said, "So you want to be a partner."

"I wouldn't stretch it that far," Slocum said. "I doubt a man like yourself wants too many partners. I'll provide a valuable service and my payment will be a percentage of the profit from the deal. A deal," he added while getting to his feet, "that you wouldn't have at all unless you either got my help or if you somehow found enough gunmen to take me out. From what I've seen so far, none of these men look half as mean as Jeremiah Hartley and we both know what happened to him."

"I'd be more than happy to have you aboard, John." With that, Dawson extended a hand, which Slocum shook. "You can start with—"

"I'll start later," Slocum said sharply.

Abel Dawson was obviously not a man who was accustomed to being brushed off like that. John Slocum, on the other hand, was a man who enjoyed turning the tables on blowhards who thought they were above such treatment. His only regret was that he couldn't see the look on Dawson's face when he turned his back to him and walked out of that office.

14

When Slocum left Dawson's office, he walked in a crisp stride, but not as if he was in a rush. Despite the calm expression he wore, every one of his senses was working to its limit to pick up any hint that things were about to go from bad to worse.

The gunmen in the hallway seemed to be doing the same thing. They watched him carefully, but didn't make any sudden moves. Every hand that had been poised above a holstered pistol was still in the same spot, although some of the tension had somehow vanished. Slocum attributed that to the heavy footsteps that had sounded behind him when he first left Dawson's office. Undoubtedly, the big man himself was watching him go and told his men what to do through silent gestures or nods.

Slocum went down to the second floor, straight to his room, and opened the door. As he turned to step inside, he caught sight of a few men standing farther down the hall. He'd only spotted them from the corner of his eye, but knew they were sent to watch him and would be there when he came back. Just to be certain nobody intended on getting any closer, Slocum closed his door and locked it. As an added precaution, he wedged a chair beneath the knob before rummaging through his saddlebags.

In the back of his mind, he cursed himself for leaving such valuable goods behind. Of course, if he had known that he would be separated from the bags for so long, he would have taken the little pouch with him. As it stood, he gave himself terrible odds that the gold would still be there at all. Surely, Dawson had sent someone to this room to sift through his belongings. Slocum was surprised that the furnishings weren't overturned and all of his things scattered on the floor. He was even more surprised when his probing hand found the pouch right where he'd left it at the bottom of the bag.

Slocum removed the bag and felt its weight in his hand. Seemed about right.

He opened it and took a look inside. "Will wonders never cease?" he muttered as he got a look at the gold nuggets inside. He had no way of knowing if some of the ore had been taken, but the fact that it was still there at all meant the saddlebags had most likely not been disturbed. Even if Dawson hadn't given the order to rob Slocum, the men who'd been eyeing him in that hotel were definitely the sorts who would help themselves if such an opportunity presented itself.

With his gold tucked away in his pocket, Slocum set about leaving his room. He wasn't about to go the way he'd come in, however. Instead, he went to his window, peeled back the curtain, and took a look outside. There was a balcony that was just wide enough to be seen without leaning outside. It sloped downward toward the street and wouldn't be much of a drop for him to get to ground level. He knew as much because the last time he'd been in town, he'd made a similar escape from a different room on the same floor of that very hotel. His window opened quietly enough, allowing Slocum to climb outside and place a foot gingerly upon the balcony.

The balcony may have been more of an awning with a flat overhang, but it was strong enough to support Slocum's weight for the second or two he needed to shimmy out to the edge and swing down. As quiet as his landing was, it would have been noticed immediately if there had been any folks on the street. Slocum turned toward the front window, which was only a few paces away from where his boots had slapped down against the dirt. The people inside were still going about their business, talking loudly and having their breakfasts without making a fuss about the man who had just dropped from overhead.

Slocum dusted himself off, straightened his hat, and walked down the street. Even after rounding the corner, he was uneasy. If Dawson had anyone posted to keep watch on the street, they couldn't miss him. Slocum was the only man walking out there, and when he spotted movement across the street, he snapped his head in that direction while dropping a hand to his holstered .44.

"Howdy," said a fellow in a butcher's apron.

Slocum nodded to him. Farther along the street, more folks emerged from various doorways, alleys, or any number of routes that brought them to Mescaline's merchant district. Most of the locals knew each other and exchanged pleasant greetings as they unlocked their doors, propped signs in their windows, and otherwise made preparations for the day to begin. For the first time since he'd been back in town, Slocum felt like he was in familiar surroundings. That taste of normalcy made it much easier to keep his head up and sort through the tangled web that he'd just created where Abel Dawson was concerned.

Navigating the streets became easier as memories rushed to fill in the gaps that had formed over time. It helped that Mescaline wasn't a large town in the first place. With all those factors coming into play, Slocum was able to make his way to the Leigensheim Brokerage Company without a single bad turn.

As far as businesses went, the brokerage company wasn't a large one. In fact, the sign with that name on it was almost wider than the office's front wall. Slocum stepped inside and found a stick of a man with straw-like hair fidgeting with one of several sets of scales.

"Making sure they're all balanced in your favor, Ed?" Slocum said good-naturedly.

The skinny fellow swiped a hand over his scalp to press down a clump of hair that promptly popped back up again. Small, dark eyes squinted toward the door, where sunlight poured through to nearly blind him. "I do *not* fix my scales, sir! You can examine any of them yourself if you do not believe me!"

Slocum walked up to the counter, which was far enough inside to shade it as well as him from the brilliant rays of light coming in through the window. "Take a breath, Ed, I was only joshing."

Now that his customer was more clearly visible, Ed took a closer look. "John Slocum? Is that you?"

"Sure enough. How's business?"

"It would be better if folks didn't spread vicious rumors about my business ethics or the quality of my scales."

"Comes with the territory," Slocum said as he hefted the weight of the pouch he'd brought from his room. "No way around it. You still get customers?"

"Enough to keep me afloat."

"Then that means people don't really take those vicious rumors very seriously."

Having spotted the pouch the instant Slocum took it out, Ed moved behind the little counter at the front of his office. He did so with a pronounced limp, wincing slightly every time his left foot touched the floor. One side of the narrow room was crowded with scales, and various charts were tacked to the walls. The counter as well as a few display cases were on the other side. Inside the cases were bits of equipment for sale, most of which were measuring tools, telescopes, or other items someone might need if they were exploring or mining. More common tools such as shovels and tin pans would have to be found elsewhere.

"I see you have brought some business of your own," Ed mused as though he could see straight through the bag to inspect its contents.

"Figured you'd give me a fair price . . . especially since I kept this office from being burnt to the ground."

"No need to remind me of that," Ed replied with a sigh. "I am reminded of Jeremiah Hartley with every step I take." He leaned forward to get closer to the bag. When his left leg accepted more of his weight, the broker let out a short, strained grunt.

If Slocum hadn't been there the day Jeremiah Hartley decided to teach Ed a lesson, he might have thought the skinny man was playing up his impediment. But Ed wasn't fooling about and neither was Hartley. The outlaw, having been upset with not getting whatever ridiculous price he'd demanded for a pair of gold teeth he'd knocked out of someone's mouth, smashed Ed's kneecap with a pickax that had been on sale at the time in Ed's inventory. He then forced the broker to walk outside on the smashed leg and do a jig in the street.

A few neighbors had tried to help Ed, but were promptly shot. That was the day that Slocum had gotten his first glimpse of Hartley at his worst. It was the day Slocum took it upon himself to put Hartley down like the mad dog he was. It was also the day Ed Leigensheim stopped selling pickaxes.

"Can I take a look?" Ed asked.

Slocum nodded and handed over the gold. "Go right ahead. That's why I'm here."

"Is it?" Now that he had the pouch in hand, had opened it, and was pouring the contents onto his countertop, Ed was only marginally invested in any conversation concerning something other than rare or valuable minerals. "You came to Mescaline only to partake of my services?"

"Yes, sir."

Ed glanced up, snorted once, and then got back to his inspection.

"What?" Slocum asked. "You think I'm lying?"

"Not as such."

"Then what's so hard to believe? I came into a handful of gold and eventually got some silver to go along with it. I was in Nevada and didn't want to get fleeced by some blowhard with shallow pockets, so I thought of my good friend Ed Leigensheim."

The squint Ed used when inspecting the gold was markedly different than the one he'd worn earlier when he simply couldn't see. "Where's the silver?"

"I ran into some trouble at Davis Junction and thought I'd try cutting my losses and heading west."

"What happened?"

"I met up with a slimy crook who probably weighted his scales with lead."

"Ahh," Ed mused. "You must be talking about Reid Flanders."

"You got that right," Slocum replied. "I figured if I wanted a proper price, I should visit an old friend."

"That is very good of you to say, Mr. Slocum, but I daresay there are better reasons for you to return to this town." Straightening his face to remove the squint that had twisted nearly all of his features, he added, "And better brokers out West."

"Better reasons, huh? You mean like Abel Dawson?"

"No. I mean like Anna Redlinger. You two had a dalliance, did you not?"

Slocum couldn't help but chuckle. "A dalliance? I suppose we did, at that."

"Then again, if you came back to have a word with Mr. Dawson, that would not be such a bad thing."

Now it was Slocum's turn to squint as he examined the man in front of him. "You say that as if you're not convinced."

"Don't get me wrong," Ed quickly replied. "I would love to see that pompous ass be taken down a notch. Then again, it is not an outsider's job to handle town business. No offense to any outsider in particular."

"None taken."

"We should never have allowed that man to declare himself mayor and enforce his edicts with threats and despicable acts against innocent souls. Whatever befalls someone after they stand by and allow that to happen . . . they deserve."

"Now that is what I call harsh," Slocum said. Since he knew all too well that Ed had a personal stake in the subject, he decided not to press it any further in that direction. "Since I'm in town, though . . ."

Ed's eyes snapped up to meet Slocum's. "You truly did not come because of Dawson?"

Slocum shook his head. "Never even heard of the man until he decided to fire the first shot against me."

"The bounty?" Ed asked with half a smirk. "He meant that to frighten anyone from trying to find you. I knew those notices would do well enough to bring you here. Many of us did. That's why we let him circulate the damndable things. Oftentimes, a man's arrogance is enough to be his downfall."

"I've learned that very same thing over the years. What can you tell me about Dawson's men?"

"Why would I have any special information in that regard?"

"Not special information, as such. Just a few specific numbers would help. A man in your profession is good at counting. A man who prospers in this field as someone who's more than a cashier is also good at noticing the fine little details. Something like that isn't just put away at the end of the day."

Ed raised an eyebrow, showing almost as much interest as he'd had for the nuggets spread out in front of him. "Perhaps."

"You might have an accurate count of how many gunmen Dawson has on his payroll."

"He does not consider them gunmen," Ed said with no small amount of disdain. "He calls them advisors and body-guards to protect him against retaliations from . . ." Scowling, he grunted. "It is a bunch of nonsense. They are gunmen, no matter what they are called."

"I hear they're not exactly cut from the same cloth as Jeremiah Hartley or the scum that rode with him."

"That is true. Some are simple gunfighters, but most are professional."

"How professional?"

"Professional enough to know it is better to fight in the dark and show a smile to a man so he can sink a knife into his back once it is turned toward him."

"Yeah," Slocum said. "That's pretty much what I've heard. No straight fights, but families are threatened and . . . worse."

Ed did not move. Suddenly, he blinked a few times and shifted his attention back to the rocks on his counter. "We have found that if we just follow a few of Dawson's rules, we can go about our lives. More or less. I suppose that is why we have grown complacent."

"More or less? You say you folks allowed this to happen, but that's not what I heard. I was told Old Man Garrett's family was attacked as well as plenty of other families of men who didn't step into line when Dawson snapped his fingers. What were you supposed to do about that?"

"Something, Mr. Slocum. I don't know, but we should have done more. I'll buy this gold from you, by the way. Come over to the scales."

Slocum followed Ed across the room, noticing how well the broker moved around once he'd gotten some steam built up. He allowed Ed to go through the process of weighing the gold while each of three separate measurements was meticulously checked three times over.

Finally, Slocum said, "I'm willing to help where Dawson is concerned."

"I know you are. You're a good man."

"You talk like you're losing your appetite for this place."

Ed nudged one of the weights on his scales. "I've lost my appetite for a great many things. That's a common ailment around here."

"You deserve a fresh start."

"Already had one. It didn't last long."

"Then let me see what I can do for my own peace of mind," Slocum said. "That pompous ass that's stretched out on the top floor of the Three Star made a show by threatening my life for all to see. Any number of men could have tried collecting that reward money. Lord knows it wouldn't have been the first time something like that has happened. Just help me see to it that it doesn't happen again where Dawson is concerned. I'd consider it a personal favor."

Although he might not have been entirely convinced that Slocum wanted to lock horns with Dawson for just that reason, Ed sighed and said, "We owe you a lot more than what you're asking."

"Then let's start there. And," Slocum added as he nodded toward the scales, "if you're feeling generous, I wouldn't mind an extra nudge on that scale favoring my payment."

Ed smiled. "I'm a grateful man, but I am also a businessman. You'll get the best price I can offer. Now what sort of numbers did you want where Dawson's men are concerned?"

"Let's start with how many there are."

"In all, I've seen a dozen. No . . . make that a baker's dozen."

"Well armed?"

"The usual," Ed said with a shrug. "Pistols. Shotguns. Nothing more than that. Always worn out in the open so they can show them to anyone who walks by."

"Why the curfew?" Slocum asked.

"Just another way to keep his herd in line."

"Usually a man who imposes his will on a bunch of folks under the auspices of looking out for them calls them his flock."

"That," Ed said sharply, "is what a preacher says. If Dawson ever tried to pass himself off as a man of God, I would shoot him myself and say to hell with those gunmen."

"Why don't you let me worry about that? What do you know about the railroad line coming through these parts?"

"What railroad line? You mean the one that goes through Davis Junction?"

"Could be a line branching off from that one or possibly some new tracks being laid down fairly soon," Slocum replied. "I don't know many details, but I do know that Dawson has got some big plans in that direction."

"There is always money to be made from that kind of knowledge," Ed mused. "Land investments. Equipment sales. There is even money to be made for someone who can point enough men to so many new jobs. Are you sure about this?"

"I pieced it together," Slocum admitted. "Nothing against this town, but I couldn't think of a good reason why a man like Dawson would try so hard to become mayor of it unless he stood to gain from it somehow. It couldn't really be a strike in one of the mines around here. Any number of men who know this desert like the back of their hand would know if that was coming. There's been rumblings of the railroad expanding through these parts. I saw some men surveying the land just outside of Davis Junction. Could have been scouts for a railroad crew."

"Could have been, eh?"

"That's right. Like I already told you, I didn't know much about it. I just figured Dawson would either be after land or gold. Only the railroad throws around enough money for land to inspire Dawson's actions. I tossed out my guess to Dawson and he gobbled it up like a hungry trout."

"Seems it is not just the miners who are granted the occasional lucky strike." Nodding, Ed motioned to the scale and asked, "Do you agree with my measurements?"

"Looks good to me. I trust you, Ed."

"And I trust you. I trust you will not get yourself killed. You were lucky enough to come out alive when you took a stand against that animal Jeremiah Hartley. Dawson is a different kind of animal. He needs to be finished all the way, until there is nothing left. He has friends, investors—who knows how many more will come here if they are called? And while he waits for them, he will chip away at whoever he can reach. Mostly, those who have nothing to do with any of this."

"I've heard he goes after what a man holds dear," Slocum said. "To weaken the man before a fight."

"And I'm sure he already knows who you hold dear, John. Just as I do. That pretty lady who works in a restaurant down the street."

"That's why I'm not about to step right up to him like I did with Hartley. When things start to happen with this, I need you to go along with it and be ready to back me up. Anyone who wants to take part in defending this town should have guns ready. Any sort of guns. Hunting rifles, pistols, whatever they can find. I don't want anyone making a stand until I make mine. If Dawson or his men ask about anything along those lines, you've just got to act as if we never had this conversation. Anyone you know, you have them do the same. Spread the word, all right? I've already had similar talks with some others."

Ed nodded as he limped back over to his money drawer for Slocum's payment. "Don't do anything stupid."

"Come now," Slocum chuckled. "You know I can't make a promise like that."

15

Slocum walked away from Leigensheim's office with an empty pouch and a tidy profit. He'd stayed with the broker for a short while after the gold was weighed, but didn't want to spend too much time there. During the rest of his conversation, he'd learned plenty about Abel Dawson. At least, it was more than enough to use in the job that was laid out in front of him.

He slowed his pace as he drew closer to the Three Star. The streets were alive with people, horses, even a few dogs by now. With them going about their lives, Mescaline felt more like a proper town instead of a cemetery. Many of the folks recognized Slocum and he acknowledged their waves or smiles with simple nods. After all, he did not want to attract attention so long as there was a chance that he could approach the Three Star without being noticed by the wrong men.

Just before he arrived at the hotel, Slocum shifted his hat forward so it covered a good portion of his face. From above, he was just another body in the crowd. He circled around the hotel to approach it from the side, where a set of stairs led up to doors on the second and third floors. From past experience, Slocum knew those doors opened to small rooms on each floor. Both were used for holding supplies when he'd been there, but he figured they were probably locked now that Dawson had claimed the hotel for himself. Slocum wasn't interested in going through any doors, however. He had his mind set on just one particular window.

Keeping his feet close to the sides of each stair as he made his way to the second floor, Slocum climbed over the railing and tentatively placed a foot upon a narrow ledge. It held his weight just fine, so he scooted along the wall until he reached the overhang skirting that portion of the building. "Should've just used the damn stairs on my way down," he grumbled.

His steps knocked too loudly against the ledge, but nobody came out to investigate. If anyone was taking notice on the street, they were keeping quiet as well. He was only exposed for about a minute before he got to his window and eased it open. His heart skipped a beat when he heard loud knocking coming from somewhere nearby.

If someone was stomping overhead, that meant they already knew what Slocum was up to and were probably on their way out to put an end to it. If they were storming out to meet him from one of the other second-floor windows, the picture didn't get any prettier. As he climbed into his room, Slocum realized it was none of those things.

"Slocum!" someone shouted from the other side of his door. The man in the hallway knocked again, his fist pounding hard enough to shake the door on its hinges. "Come on out of there before I break this door down!"

When the pounding started anew, Slocum shut the window and tugged at his shirt so it was partly unbuttoned as well as partly untucked from his jeans. After pulling the chair away from the door, he finally opened it. "What the hell is wrong with you?" he groaned.

The man who'd been knocking was one of the shotgunners that had been lounging on the third floor, but Slocum didn't recall hearing his name. He poked his nose into the room, took a quick look, and then asked, "What were you doing?"

"Sleeping. What do you think?"

"You already got up and had breakfast."

"I was also drinking enough whiskey last night that I could stand to sleep a bit more," Slocum explained. "Not that it's any of your business."

"You didn't hear us knocking?"

"I opened the door, didn't I?"

"Why was it blocked shut?" the shotgunner asked.

Without hesitation, Slocum replied, "Why were you trying to bust in?"

The shotgunner studied him carefully. "What about when we tried to fetch you before?"

"When was that?"

"About ten minutes ago."

Slocum shrugged. "Must've been some good whiskey. Know what I mean?"

If the shotgunner knew, he wasn't going to say as much. "Mr. Dawson wants a word with you. Your horse in the stable out back?"

"Yeah. If I need it right quick, you can go saddle it for me."

Slocum's guess was that it would take another jibe or two to get the younger man to charge inside and grab hold of him. When he did so after that comment, Slocum was almost surprised.

Almost.

As soon as the shotgunner moved forward, Slocum rushed to meet him. That way, he caught the other man in mid-stride when he was off balance and perfectly set up for a fall. Slocum grabbed the shotgun in his hands and turned it in a tight semicircle. The younger man attempted to hang on to his weapon for as long as possible, but was unable to do so once his wrists were ground together and his arms were twisted like two strings of taffy. From there, all that was left was for him to bang a shoulder against the door frame and allow his weapon to be taken from him. Rather than do anything to rattle any of the other men in the hall, Slocum strode out and handed the shotgun to the next guard he saw.

"Keep this for me," he said idly, "and get me some coffee. Is Dawson waiting for me upstairs?"

"Yes," one of the other men said. Although he'd just seen his partner handled so efficiently, he was now holding an extra shotgun and didn't seem to have anything to fear from the man who'd humiliated his friend. Besides, Slocum had now reached the staircase and was already out of his sight.

The first shotgunner had collected himself by this point and stormed out to grab his weapon. "Glad you were along," he sneered to the other guard. All that one could do was shrug.

Slocum dashed up the stairs with a spry step that brought him to the third floor before his presence could be announced. Dawson was on his way back to his office carrying a cup of tea in his hands while wearing a surprised expression on his face. "Where have you been, John?" he asked.

"Getting some more sleep," Slocum replied. "I had a feeling I'd need to be rested up."

"You were right on that account. Come into my office so I can have a word with you."

Slocum followed him to his office, but didn't go all the way inside. Instead, he stood in the doorway, where he could watch Dawson as well as the other men on the third floor. At the moment, there were only a trio of guards walking idly between rooms.

"Come on in," Dawson urged. "All the way in and shut the door."

Slocum did as he was asked, but kept the door open a crack so he could hear what was going on outside and get out quickly if the need arose.

Already behind his desk, Dawson said, "You still serious about working for me?"

"I'm still here, ain't I?"

"Yes, indeed. Someone's come along to back up your claim about that grisly business in Davis Junction. I want you to accompany a couple of my men down there to find out why that man was killed. You say it was just for speaking up on my behalf?"

"That's what I said," Slocum replied.

"Then I want you to find out what he said to spark such a reaction."

"Anything else you'd like me to do for you while I'm there?" Slocum asked. "Maybe I could bring you back something to eat?"

"You want to work for me? You'll do the work I give you."

"I believe I wanted to work with you," Slocum pointed out.

Wearing the same crooked smile that had been plastered onto his face most of the time that Slocum had seen him, Dawson said, "Then work with me . . . and go to Davis Junction to see what happened with that killing. I'd appreciate it."

"See, now that's all I needed. Just a little courtesy." Slocum tipped his hat. "I'll have a look at your men to see which ones I want to take with me."

"Already have 'em picked out. They're waiting for you in the lobby."

Standing just outside the office, Slocum turned to look back in as he asked, "Does the work get any better than this?"

"Most definitely! I just need to see what kind of a worker you are. After that, I promise I'll give you so much rewarding work to do that you'll be glad those little notices I drew up brought you here."

"Yeah. I'm sure." Slocum walked down the stairs, ignoring all the men who watched him from various doorways. When he started counting them, he realized there weren't as many as he'd originally thought. The simple fact was that those men were always watching from the confined quarters of the narrow hallway, which made their numbers seem greater. It was similar to how a toy soldier could look like a giant if it was held close enough to the eye. Now that he had some proper perspective, Slocum decided Ed's figures probably weren't far off. He shook his head and silently scolded himself for doubting the broker's numbers. More than likely, any figure that man tossed out had already been checked and double-checked.

Ever since he'd climbed back in through his window, Slocum had been trying to gauge whether or not any of Dawson's men knew he'd been gone. Judging from his limited conversations with Dawson, Slocum had no trouble at all believing the man was so overly confident that he might not consider the possibility he'd been duped. Men like that always figured they had eyes in the back of their head and enough brains to figure out whatever they couldn't see. On the other hand, it could be just as likely that Slocum's little walk to Ed's place hadn't fooled anyone and the others were merely playing along. All that mattered was that Slocum knew where he stood and didn't get overconfident himself.

When he saw the men waiting in the lobby for him, he could tell it was going to be a long ride to Davis Junction.

The first man Slocum spotted was Mikey. His face actually looked worse than it had earlier that day. The bruises had taken on the color of muddy swamp water flowing just beneath his skin. His eyes narrowed into angry slits and he placed his hand squarely upon the grip of his holstered pistol when he saw Slocum coming. "Well now," he said. "Look who decided to join us after his little catnap."

"If you boys don't mind waiting awhile, I could sure use a bit more sleep," Slocum said.

"Get your ass onto a horse before I—"

In an instant, Slocum surged forward to stand so close to Mikey that he could bump his forehead with the brim of his hat. "You'll what?" he snarled. All of the glibness that had been in his voice a second ago had now been replaced with the steely chill of a cold blade.

"Easy, now," one of the other men said. He was a bony kid who couldn't have seen more than twenty-one birthdays. The grip he applied to Slocum's shoulder was strong enough to ease him away from Mike, but not more than half a step. Slocum shifted his glare to him and found little fear in the younger man's smooth features.

All Slocum needed to do to get the kid's hand to move away was to look at it as if he meant to cut it off. After that, he met the kid's pale green eyes and asked, "You leading this ride, Slim?"

"Don't know if there's a proper leader. We're all just headed down to Davis Junction to look into that matter you told Mr. Dawson about."

"What matter would that be?" Slocum asked.

Slim shifted uncomfortably from one foot to another before the third man spoke up. He was a stocky Mexican with a bushy mustache that was long enough to cover most of his mouth as he said, "We're looking into the death of one of Mr. Dawson's supporters."

Slocum nodded, comfortable in the knowledge that he'd just found the group's leader. "Any idea how we do that, or do we just ride into town and start knocking on doors?"

"We know plenty of men to ask, but you're coming along on this to point us in the right direction."

"I suppose we can talk about strategy when we make camp tonight," Slocum said.

"Camp? What camp?"

"Davis Junction isn't far from here, but it's a bit late to get there in less than a day's ride."

"Not if we ride at night," Mike said. "Seems like maybe you don't know as much as you thought."

"Shut up," the Mexican snapped. "Both of you."

"You think you can make the ride without stopping?"

Slocum said. "Go right ahead. I'll just get some supplies in the event it takes longer."

"I've made the ride more times than I can count," the large, dark-skinned man replied. "I know how long it will take. We'll be making the last part of the ride at night, but that don't matter either. We'll get to work as soon as we arrive."

Slocum nodded slowly. "Yeah, I've heard you men do your best work at night."

"Don't forget that," Mike said. When he saw the glare he got from the Mexican, he added, "And don't shove me around, Sanchez! I know what I'm doing."

"Then do it!" Sanchez bellowed. "The horses are outside. We've wasted enough time already."

Sanchez led the way out of the hotel and the other two men fell into step in front of and behind Slocum. They filed through the front door, marching straight to the horses tethered to the closest post. Slocum's gelding was saddled and had a canteen hanging by a strap, but little else. "Where's the rest of my gear?" he asked.

"You've got what you need," Sanchez replied. "We've got the rest. Are you coming or not?"

Slocum knew that question was as loaded as the guns all three men were carrying. More than likely, some men inside the hotel were watching from other spots, waiting for a reason to open fire. His muscles drew taut beneath his skin, aching to make a move of his own, but Slocum forced himself to climb into his saddle as if he didn't have a care in the world.

The other three mounted their horses and, within seconds, were trotting down the street toward the edge of town. Once the desert was spread in front of them, Sanchez snapped his reins. Slocum followed with the other two on either side of him.

16

They rode like the wind for the rest of the day. Several times, Slocum thought it was more fitting to say they rode like a wind being pushed in front of a storm with an even bigger wind behind it. The ground they covered was familiar at first, but Sanchez quickly veered off onto a trail that Slocum had never seen before. It seemed to be broken in several places, but when any other rider might have turned back to look for a safer route, Sanchez pressed on.

Just when it seemed the horses would collapse from lack of water, Sanchez brought them to a stop near a watering hole that was so small it could have gone unnoticed by anyone who didn't already know it was there. They let the horses drink, refilled their canteens, and pressed on.

Sunlight baked the desert without the slightest bit of pity or remorse for those who rode beneath it. As the evening approached, Slocum felt the air grow cooler and somewhat more bearable. When the skies became filled with orange and purple hues, the wind soothed his sweating face instead of raking it with hot iron claws. Not long after that, the air grew icy teeth and the entire desert became colder. Overhead, stars were spread like diamond flecks drifting on a sea of inky water. Slocum became increasingly nervous as the ground in front of him became harder and harder to see. And despite the fact that the terrain itself had become a danger, they pressed on.

The first thing Slocum spotted was the train depot. It sat at the edge of Davis Junction like a sleeping beast illuminated by rows of lanterns situated along the tracks leading into town. Soon, his eyes picked out the smaller beacons of windows illuminated from the inside by cooking fires, candles, or lanterns within homes and saloons. Slocum's eyes quickly became adjusted to the darkness surrounding him, allowing him to make out the shape of a cabin directly ahead. Sanchez and the others reined their horses to a stop outside that cabin and quickly dismounted.

"Is there any food inside?" Slocum asked. "I'm about ready to eat one of you if I don't get something in my stomach."

"There's food inside," Slim told him. "It ain't much, but it's better than nothing."

Slocum followed them into the cabin while Sanchez lit a single lantern hanging from a hook on the wall. The sputtering light cast twitching shadows upon several crates stacked in a corner, a few barrels, some sacks of oats, and a pile of smaller boxes beneath a thick blanket. Mike was the one who peeled away the blanket and tore into one of the boxes. He whooped in glee when he found a bundle of jerked meat and canned beans, which he divvied out among Sanchez and Slim.

"What about me?" Slocum asked.

"You got two hands," Mike grunted. "Help yerself."

Once the others had moved aside, Slocum rummaged in the opened box and found more of the same. The jerked meat tasted like salty rabbit, but it sated him as he gnawed on it before helping himself to a can of beans. When he turned away from the boxes, Sanchez tossed something at him from the doorway. At first the metal thing coming at him looked like a blade, so Slocum leaned over to clear a path for it. The thing clanged against another stack of boxes and rattled to the floor near his boot. Slocum bent down, picked it up, and examined it. The can opener was innocent enough, so he nodded to the Mexican and said, "Much obliged."

"Who's this man that was supposed to have been killed?" Sanchez asked.

"Oh, he was killed all right. He worked at one of the stables in town. I believe his name was Derrick."

"And he was killed for speaking on Mr. Dawson's behalf?"

"That's what I heard."

"What did he say that got him killed? Plenty of folks around here know Mr. Dawson and they don't have a problem with him."

"I don't know what he said," Slocum replied. "I wasn't there when the poor bastard was killed. I know where it happened, though, and I know who to talk to for a few answers."

"Don't worry about talking to anyone unless I ask you to talk," Sanchez said.

It was all Slocum could do to keep from knocking the Mexican onto his ass right then and there. Instead of following through with such an appealing idea, he said, "I'm just here to lend a hand. If you want my opinion, though, it might be best if nobody knew I was with you."

"Why's that?"

"Because I asked a few questions myself before I left and the answers I got were nothing but a pile of bullshit."

"What were you told?"

"I asked what happened," Slocum said, "and the sheriff just told me it was some sort of drunken fight that went from bad to worse. I know that's not the case. If I go in there again, we might get that same load of manure thrown at us. I'd rather not waste any time with that."

"You're coming with us, Slocum," Sanchez insisted. "That's not a matter of discussion."

Slocum held up his hands as if he were being robbed. Then he reached around his neck to untie the bandanna he'd been wearing for the entire ride. He wrapped the bandanna over his nose and mouth, tied it in the back, and then lowered his hands. "This should be enough to let me ride with you men without causing any unnecessary commotion with the local law."

"Fine," Sanchez grunted. "If you need to eat, do it quickly. We're heading into town as soon as we can."

When Slocum pulled down the bandanna, he was smiling agreeably. That lasted until Sanchez left the cabin. His first order of business was to open that can as quickly as possible so he could shovel as many beans into his mouth before the ride continued.

They rode through Davis Junction like a band of outlaws. Nobody looked shiftier than Slocum since he kept a tight grip on his reins, his head down, and his eyes darting back and forth above the mask he wore.

"Where should we start?" Sanchez asked him.

Pointing toward the stable situated farthest away from the sheriff's office, Slocum replied, "Right there. But let me go in first."

"I thought you wanted to lay low."

"I will. I just need to take a quick look around to see if there's anyone in there we need to worry about."

"Who do you mean?"

"I don't know their names!" Slocum snapped. "I only know them on sight. If you don't want to let me do anything, then just cut me loose and I can get a comfortable bed for the night."

Mike started to react, but was held back by Sanchez's raised hand. "Fine," the Mexican said. "You go in first, but we'll be right behind you. Come back out right away and let me know what you saw."

"Fair enough." With that, Slocum snapped his reins and

rode to the stable. He listened for any horses riding directly behind him, but it seemed Sanchez was as good as his word and hanging back for now.

There was a hint of light from inside the stable. As Slocum got closer, he could see the light bobbing and swaying as its source within the structure kept moving. He swung down from his saddle and hurried toward the front door. Before he could get close enough to try its handle, the door was opened by the stable's solitary keeper.

"What do you want?" Vivienne asked. Once she got a better look at the masked figure coming toward her, she said, "We're full up. Go somewhere else."

Slocum reached out for her, which caused her to retreat even faster. Before she could scream, he pressed his hand flat against her mouth and pushed her inside. Once he'd kicked the door shut, Slocum pulled the bandanna away from his face and told her, "It's me. Don't scream."

She still seemed ready to scream, but stopped herself after the sight of him sank in. "John! What are you doing here?"

"There are men coming and they're hot on my heels. What's happened in regard to the man that was killed?"

Vivienne wrapped her arms around him and squeezed. "They're saying you did it."

"On what grounds?"

"I don't know," she replied while vehemently shaking her head. "Maybe because you rode off when you were supposed to stay and answer for what happened."

"Who was he?"

"Just some stable hand."

Slocum grabbed her by both arms and held her in front of him so he could look her in the eyes when he asked, "Who was he, Vivienne?"

"Why would I know?"

"Because you know plenty of men who stumble into some very unfortunate circumstances."

"I . . . like dangerous men," she said with a shrug.

"Always have. When you came in here just now, looking the way you did . . . could you put that mask back on?"

Even with everything that was going on, Slocum found it hard to resist the hungry look in her eyes. It was even harder for him to say, "If you like dangerous men so much, then you'll love the ones that are behind me. I need you to do something."

"And I need you to do something for me," she purred. "Right now."

"There are three men coming," he said. "I need you to keep at least one of them busy."

"How?"

Slocum pulled the bandanna back up over his nose so it covered the lower portion of his face. "Come now," he said. "Don't tell me you don't know how to keep a man preoccupied for a little while?"

"For how long?" she asked.

"As long as you can. I'll come along to fetch him later. Just make sure he doesn't leave this stable and *don't* let on that you know me. If anyone else you know comes along, just send them on their way without mentioning a word about me being here."

She nodded vigorously. "Tell me what's going on, John. It sounds so exciting!"

"If you know anything about the man that was killed," he said, "now's the time to tell me."

"But I don't—"

"Right now," he said sternly.

At first, Vivienne looked as if she would maintain her innocent posturing. When she lowered her head, Slocum knew he was wrong to think she wasn't a part of what had happened. "I knew Derrick for a while," she told him. "He followed me around like a lost little pup and Wendell didn't like it. Didn't like it at all."

"Who's Wendell?"

"He owns the other stable in town. I left there on account

of him thinking he owned me like I was one of them horses he brushes every other night. Wendell put his hands on me a few times, but I would rather spend my time with Derrick. He was younger and stronger and taller. One night, Wendell found us together and he went crazy."

"How long ago was this?" Slocum asked.

"Maybe a month."

"So what's that got to do with Derrick getting killed?"

"Maybe nothing," she said with a shrug. "You asked if I knew anything more about Derrick and that's all I know. Well . . . all I know that would be of any help."

The other horses were approaching. Slocum could hear them slowing as they drew closer to the stable. Making certain the bandanna was in place, he said, "Remember what I told you, Viv. It's important."

"I remember. I'll do just like you said."

Although Slocum wasn't completely certain he could trust her, there wasn't any time to second-guess the instincts that had brought him this far. It was too late to turn back now.

Moments after the horses came to a stop, Sanchez and Mike were stepping into the stable. They eyed Slocum suspiciously before turning their attention to the blond woman standing there. "Hello, Vivienne," Sanchez said.

She nodded and averted her eyes.

Slocum glared at her, wondering how much more she'd forgotten to mention. Then again, he hadn't mentioned exactly who was with him or if she might have known them.

"We're at the wrong stable," Slocum said.

The Mexican looked over at him. "You sure about that?"

"The man that was killed worked at the one on the other side of town."

"If you're looking for people who knew him," Vivienne said, "then you might want to stay here as well. Sometimes a few of his friends come by."

Mike jumped in to say, "I'll stay here and wait." When Sanchez looked over at him, he added, "The man worked at a stable, right? Isn't too much of a stretch to think that someone we might want to talk to could show up at this one, right? Besides, I think this lady has some more to say to me that she didn't tell our . . . friend over there."

Sanchez let out a slow breath. "Stay here with the horses," he said. "Keep them ready to go at a moment's notice. Understand?" When Mike didn't answer right away, he snapped, "Understand?"

"I heard you the first time," Mike replied. "I know how to do my damn job."

"Make sure of it. And you'd best be ready to do your job when the time comes."

"Trust me. It won't be a problem."

To Vivienne, Sanchez said, "There was a man killed here recently. Who was he?"

"Derrick Sloane," she said. "He worked at the stable across town. If you want to know who killed him, have a word with the man who owns that place. If Wendell didn't put the knife in himself, I bet he knows who did."

"Why was Derrick killed?"

Slocum's stomach tightened into a knot. He hadn't gotten a chance to tell her how to answer that question. One slip now could pose a mighty big problem.

She looked around at the three men in front of her. Two anxiously stared back at her, and the third was hungrily staring at her ample breasts. Finally, she shrugged and said, "I don't know why he was killed. How could I know such a thing?"

Her ignorance was such a well-practiced act that it was immediately accepted by Sanchez. The Mexican nodded and said, "Mikey, stay put and be ready to back us up if things get rough. I'll fire a shot if we need you. Do you know where the other stables are?"

"Sure I do," he said without taking his eyes off Vivienne. "I been here before."

She smiled and brushed a hand against his chest to run

it all the way down to his gun belt. "Have you? I would think I'd remember something like that."

"Oh, I'll give you somethin' to remember me by, darlin'," Mike said.

"Listen for that shot," Sanchez said. "Otherwise, you might as well come along with us."

Mike waved them off. "You go on ahead. I'll be fine right here."

Sanchez slapped Slocum on the shoulder to get him moving toward the door. Outside, Slim waited with the horses. Even in the shadows, the nervousness on his face was easy to read.

"What did you say to that woman before we got here?" Sanchez asked.

"Just asked her where we could find anyone connected to that killing," Slocum replied. "She pointed me toward that other stable, just like I said. There's supposed to be a man named Wendell who works there that should be able to tell us a thing or two."

"Wendell has always been a good man," Slim said. "He's helped us a couple of times."

"Maybe not as good as you think," Slocum offered.

Sanchez climbed into his saddle. "Let's have a word with him before we jump to any conclusions. You just keep your mouth shut unless I ask you a question. Understand?"

"Sure do," Slocum said while fighting the impulse to say anything else.

They crossed town to the stable that was closest to the sheriff's office. Slocum watched how both Sanchez and Slim reacted and could tell they became more tightly wound as they got closer to the dimly lit window marked with the sheriff's name. When they got to the stable, Sanchez rode all the way around to the back of the building before dismounting and walking toward a narrow door.

Sanchez pounded on the door with his fist, listened for a few seconds, and then pounded some more.

"What the hell is it at this hour?" someone asked from the other side of the door. By the sound of the voice, the man asking the question had either drunk an entire bottle of firewater or had recently been punched in the throat.

"Open the door," Sanchez demanded.

"You renting a stall here?"

"No."

"Then go away. Ain't no more spaces to be had."

Sanchez lowered his voice to a growl as he said, "We're here on behalf of Abel Dawson."

The door came open a crack, which was just enough for Slocum to glimpse a single eye peering out at them from within the stable. "Mr. Dawson?" the man asked. "What's he want?"

"He doesn't like what he's heard about that Derrick fella getting killed."

"Why's he care about that?"

"Doesn't concern you," Sanchez replied. "Is Wendell inside?"

"N-No. He's at his home. Probably in bed."

"Take us to him."

"But . . . can't it wait until morning?"

Sanchez placed a hand upon the door and slowly, insistently, forced it open. "Take us to him. If you want to keep all of your teeth, you should be damn quick about it."

The man stepped outside. He was a short, elderly fellow with wisps of gray hair sprouting at irregular intervals from his scalp. His eyes were covered in a cloudy, cream-colored film, and his entire body was trembling as he pointed toward a house less than a hundred paces from the back end of the stable. "He's right in there," he said. "Go on and see for yourself."

17

Vivienne's hands brushed along Mike's bruises as if they were works of art splattered upon a canvas. "What happened to you?" she asked.

"I had some business to handle," he said. "Some men need to be taught some manners and I'm just the one to give the lesson."

Stepping up close to him, she placed her hand upon the gun strapped to his side and stroked the grip lovingly. "Did you have to kill anyone?"

"Killin' a man ain't no small thing," he told her. "It scars a man all the way down to the soul."

"You poor thing."

Mike wrapped an arm around her and drew her in close. He put his mouth at the nape of her neck and kissed her more like he was tasting her skin as his hand wandered down her back. The moment he was able to feel the slope of her buttocks through the fabric of her dress, he grabbed her tighter.

Vivienne didn't try to get away, but she did struggle to catch her breath. After less than a minute of that, she was roughly pushed away. She staggered backward until her shoulders bumped against the frame of one of the stalls, and she let out her breath in a loud gasp.

"I've seen you a few times, haven't I?" Mike asked. "When me and some of the boys have come to town on business for Mr. Dawson?"

"What kind of business do you do for him?"

Studying her carefully like any other simple-minded animal circling its prey, Mike said, "Collecting on debts mostly. Sometimes it can get rough."

"What happens then?" she asked as her cheeks flushed with color.

"If they get rough, I just have to make sure to be rougher than the other man." When Mike placed his hand upon his gun, he could tell Vivienne was watching intently and growing more excited. "Them other times I've seen you, it took me a long time to stop thinking about you."

"Did it?"

He nodded and stalked forward, keeping one hand on his gun while reaching out with the other to feel the curve of her hip. That hand worked its way up to her bosom, and when he cupped her breast, Vivienne arched her back slightly as if to make sure he could feel all of her. She even slid one leg out so that it brushed against his growing erection.

"I know I've seen you a few times," he said, "and each time I wanted you more than the last."

"You want to be inside me?" she purred. "Grab me and have your way with me?"

"Hell yes."

"I suppose . . . you being the kind of man you are . . . that there wouldn't be much I could do to stop you."

Mike placed both hands on her, which caused Vivienne to gasp again as an excited tremor worked through her body. He groped her breasts at first, massaging them and looking down at the way the cotton of her top clung to her sweaty skin. He then looked into her eyes as if waiting for a protest when he reached down to feel her hips and backside. Instead of any sign of reservation, she closed her eyes and smiled while slowly writhing in his grasp.

"Don't make me wait for it," she whispered.

That was more than enough to push Mike over the edge. He immediately unbuckled his gun belt and let it drop to the floor. His pants were next and he couldn't get out of them fast enough. He yanked them down so they were gathered around his boots, freeing his stiff cock.

Vivienne looked down at his penis and started to reach for it, but was quickly turned around to face the gate of the stall where she'd been standing. From there, Mike pulled up her skirts and began fumbling at her undergarments, looking for any way to get to the treasure he knew was beneath them. Vivienne bent forward and grabbed hold of the gate, taking a wider stance and allowing her head to hang forward so her long blond hair brushed against both sides of her face.

Mike reached in to find the smooth, bare skin of one leg. He followed that upward to her thigh. Then, he reached around to her inner thigh before finally discovering the thatch of wet hair between her legs. Every time his fingers moved against the subtle curves of her pussy, Vivienne trembled. When he dared to slip a finger inside her, she grabbed the wooden railing in front of her even harder and spread her legs wider.

Unable to contain himself a second longer, Mike hiked her skirts up around her waist before ripping a few pieces of clothing that weren't moving the way he wanted them to. After a short struggle, he'd exposed her ass and legs and was moving in place behind her.

"Is this what you thought about when you saw me?" she asked.

Mike guided his rigid pole between her thighs, pressing its tip against her wet slit. "Yes. Damn, you feel good."

She smiled and eased herself back to take him in. "There

are a few things you could maybe help me with," she sighed as he continued to slip inside her. "A big, strong man like you could fix some problems for me and I'd be so grateful."

Now that he was partially in her, Mike grabbed her hips and pumped the rest of the way between her legs. He buried his cock into her and let out a long, satisfied breath. "Anything you want, darlin'," he sighed.

"I just want you for now," she said. "Give it to me. Give it to me good and hard. I can tell the rest to you later and. . . . you can bring it up with Mr. Dawson."

Holding her firmly, Mike pounded into her again and again. His hands wandered along the smooth, firm curves of her buttocks before sliding up along the small of her back. When he eased up a bit, Vivienne rocked back and forth as if she was the one in charge of the entire situation.

"Grab my hair," she said.

Mike's hand fumbled against her back as he struggled to concentrate on more than one thing at a time. He grabbed a handful of her blond hair and gave it a tug. She reared her head back and moaned softly, urging him to follow up. When he pulled her hair again, he drove his rod in as deep as it could go.

"Damn!" she squealed. "That's it!"

Mike reached around with his free hand to grope her breast while continuing to slide in and out of her. Eventually, both hands wound up on her shoulders so he could hold her in place as he thrust with mounting urgency. His eyes were shut tightly and his muscles were tense. That changed quickly when Vivienne eased away so his penis slipped completely out of her.

He was about to say something before she wheeled around and grabbed him by the front of his shirt and put his back against the gate she'd been using for support. Mike was too shocked to react, so he tried unsuccessfully to speak as she stood in front of him and placed one foot up on the gate beside him. Her pussy glistened with moisture and was spread open wide. She reached down, guided him into her, and started grinding.

She looked deeply into his eyes as if she owned him. At that moment, both of them knew that he would have gladly followed through on any command she'd given. Vivienne only allowed him to pump into her a few more times before she stepped back once more. This time, she lowered herself to her knees and wrapped her mouth around his pole. Her lips pressed tightly against him, and she sucked loudly as her head bobbed back and forth.

"J-Jesus!" Mike said as he squirmed uncomfortably. It didn't take long for her to find a rhythm that suited him, and once she did, he kept her there by putting his hands on either side of her head and holding her in position.

Vivienne gazed up and opened her mouth wide. She eased her tongue out to slide along the bottom of his shaft as his rigid member eased back and forth between her moist lips. She ran her hands along his legs while taking him all the way into her mouth. As soon as his body started to shake, she knew she had him.

She sucked him vigorously. Her tongue swirled around his erection, and she closed her lips on it as if she were feasting on a stick of candy. Before long, his grip around her head tightened, and he started bucking against her face.

"Don't you stop, darlin'," he grunted. "Keep it up."

Instead of continuing what she was doing, Vivienne used the tip of her tongue to tease the head of his cock as she encircled her lips around him and started to make a low purring sound at the back of her throat. A few seconds of that was all it took to rush him toward a climax. Mike's back arched and he let out a rough, grunting moan. Vivienne eased her lips all the way down to the base of his cock, keeping her tongue flat against him, and by the time she eased her head back again, he was exploding into her mouth.

She drank him down and dabbed at the corner of her lips as she stood up in front of him. A wide, sly grin appeared on her face as she walked toward a bucket and ladle for a drink of water.

Hitching up his pants, Mike nodded as if he'd just completed some sort of monumental task. "We should'a done that a whole lot earlier."

"Yes, indeed."

"You ever need anything . . . anything at all . . . you just let ol' Mikey know."

"I'm sure I can think of a few things," she replied. "Like . . . do you think you could get me in to see Mr. Dawson?"

Sanchez and Slim stood in a parlor that was filled with books, a wide brick fireplace, tools needed to tend to the flames, and a stack of chopped wood collected in a wide brass rack. Wendell was in a pair of rumpled trousers that he'd just pulled on to answer the insistent pounding on his front door. The nightshirt that he'd been sleeping in was hastily tucked into half of his trousers and the other half hung out in a disheveled mess of wrinkled fabric. Strands of dark hair stuck out at odd angles while other pieces had been plastered down by hasty swipes from a hand that was now nervously fidgeting with a pocket watch that lay open on top of a small round table.

"If you wanted to have a talk with me, you could have let me know earlier," Wendell said. "We could have set up a proper time. I would have served a meal. Maybe offered you a drink."

"You can still offer me a drink," Sanchez said in a voice that was just as smooth as Wendell was rumpled.

"What do you want?" Wendell asked. "And who's he?"

Slocum stood near the doorway. His bandanna wasn't pulled all the way up over his nose, but was arranged in such a way that it still covered a good portion of his face. The shadows in the room and his distance from Wendell made certain he wasn't on prominent display.

"Don't worry about him," Sanchez said. "I'd be more worried about myself if I were you."

"Why? Mr. Dawson and I have been on good terms," Wendell said quickly. "Been that way ever since I told him about what those railroad men said when they boarded their horses at my stable. Don't forget I'm one of the first men to bring that deal to his attention."

Sanchez stood with both thumbs hooked over his gun belt. Although he wasn't making a move toward either of the two pistols he wore, he could skin the smoke wagons with minimum effort and everyone in that room knew it. "Nobody's forgotten anything," he said. "Especially me. That's why I was so shocked to hear your name mentioned in connection to the death of that stable hand."

For a second, Wendell merely blinked. Dumbfounded, he asked, "You mean Derrick?"

Sanchez nodded.

"What the hell's he got to do with anything?"

"Word is that you may know who killed him."

Wendell stormed forward about a step and a half before he collected himself and said, "The *word* is that a man by the name of John Slocum killed him. He was sniffing around that whore who works in the other stable across town."

Slocum felt his heart race and his hand drift toward his .44. Nobody seemed to be paying him any attention, but he felt as if every eye were trained on him when he eased his hand back again.

"Derrick used to sniff under them same skirts as well," Wendell continued. "Back when she worked for me, the two of them got real close. I warned him about that bitch, but he never listened. Once she let him get a taste of that honey she offers to damn near anyone with a pecker between his legs, Derrick was putty in her hands."

"Why would she care about using a stable hand?" Sanchez asked.

"Because Derrick could get to the strongbox where I keep

my profits," Wendell said. "Thing is, even after it was clear she was just after my money, he never let her be. Even after she started working at the other stable, he would call on her every chance he got."

Slim hadn't said much since Slocum had met him, but now the young gunman couldn't help but ask, "What's a lady like that doing working at a stable? I seen her once when she was working for you and it was strange enough. Having her work for another stable just don't make sense."

"It does if no one else in town will have her," Wendell replied. "She's a lying, filthy whore and the only other job she could get in town would be on her back behind a saloon. But she thinks she's too good for that. Knowing her, she probably thinks she can make more money swindling the men that come in and out of this town. Lately, as I already told Mr. Dawson, there's been plenty of railroad scouts and business types coming to Davis Junction looking to see how best to lay the tracks in that new route meant to head up north from here through Mescaline and beyond. Viv spends as much time as she can working them stables because every man that comes through here has a horse that needs to be put up. The only thing that keeps her from working the stagecoach station is because she gets chased away like a common trollop."

"Sounds to me like you've got some pretty strong opinions about her," Sanchez said. "Did she get to your cash box when she was with Derrick?"

Wendell turned and flapped a hand back at the men in his parlor while saying, "Hell no, she didn't! As for now, I couldn't give a damn what she does or who she does it to."

"Pretty rare that a man spits so much venom at someone he doesn't give a damn about. Did you ever taste any of that honey for yourself?"

When he spun around and came at Sanchez, Wendell didn't even notice how close he was to getting shot. Sanchez took hold of a pistol and so did the younger man behind him. Even Slocum reflexively drew his .44 when Wendell charged at them with so much fire in his eyes.

"That ain't none of your concern!" Wendell snarled.

Sanchez nodded slowly. "Seems like I struck a nerve. Also, there's the fact that you still call her Viv, and when you talk about her dalliances with other men, you seem more angry than disgusted. You still hold a soft spot in your heart for that whore?"

After his eyes darted toward the stairs leading up to the room where his wife slept, Wendell hissed, "Don't call her that."

"What's going on between the two of you?" Sanchez asked.

Wendell seemed ready to stay angry for as long as the men were in his house. Then he let out a breath that deflated his entire chest and allowed his head to hang forward. "Come outside," he said quietly.

All of them stepped outside, but Wendell acted as if it was only he and Sanchez standing on the front porch. The only acknowledgment he gave to Slocum or Slim was when he offered them all cigars. Slocum took his and stepped back once it was lit so he could savor the tobacco while the messy affair was sorted out.

There was a fence surrounding Wendell's house, which was where he led the others. Propping his leg up on the lowest rail, he puffed on the cigar. Glowing red embers burned brightly to cast a few shadows across his face. He held on to the smoke and let it go before quietly saying, "That little blond filly working in my stable is the sweetest thing I ever did see. She's softer than heaven itself and tastes just as sweet. I heard a few bad things about her, but that was never enough to keep any man away once she got a hold of him."

"So she's wrapped up in this killing?" Sanchez asked.

After taking another puff, Wendell nodded. "I heard how she wrapped men around her little finger. Made them do things. Made them give her money. Well . . . I suppose she didn't force them, but when she asked for something, it just didn't seem possible to say no. As far as what she's doing in stables, it's like I said before. Ain't no other place in town would hire her and she needed to earn her keep somehow after being run out of a few other towns."

"Did she kill that stable hand?"

The cigar glowed again, but Wendell stood so still that it seemed a statue was smoking it. He brought his hand up to his face, took the cigar from between his lips, lifted his head, and sent a stream of fragrant smoke toward the starry night sky. "No," he said in a voice that was colder than the chilled desert breeze. "I killed him."

"Because of her?"

Wendell nodded. "Me and her have been getting together again recently. I knew it was because of the money I've been getting from my dealings with Mr. Dawson and the whole railroad affair, but I didn't care. It was worth it just to get my hands on that fine, smooth skin. Damn, she's an angel." As if he was receiving a message from above, he moved his eyes away from the stars and admitted, "Maybe not an angel, but I sure hope there aren't any devils as tempting as Viv."

"We heard Derrick was killed because he spoke up on Mr. Dawson's behalf," Sanchez said.

Once Wendell started shaking his head, he didn't seem able to stop. "I don't know what you heard. When I killed Derrick, it was a twitch reflex. He was on his way to climb all over Viv and made sure I knew about it. I just picked up the knife and started stabbing him. I . . . couldn't stop. I just kept on stabbing until that boy was a big, bloody mess. I went and found the sheriff to tell him some damn story or other. All those lawmen had been going on about a man by the name of Slocum, and it was clear the sheriff didn't think much of this fella, so I said he was the one that killed Derrick. After that . . . I don't rightly know what I said."

Slim stepped up and asked, "You think you may have just tossed in some lie about Mr. Dawson to cover your own hide?"

"No!" Wendell said with absolute certainty. "What I mean is that I was just trying to point the sheriff's nose somewhere else. With him all bothered about Slocum, it was easy enough. Derrick used to be a good friend of mine. That's why it cut so deep when he put his hands on Vivienne."

"Sounds like plenty of men put their hands on her," Sanchez grunted.

It seemed the angry fire that had been in Wendell's eyes had burned itself out because there was none left when he shifted his gaze skyward once again. "Yeah," he replied. "It does seem that way. The sheriff and his deputy probably did some speculating of their own in regards to Derrick's connection to me and my friendship with Mr. Dawson. Word gets spread, rumors gain steam, they take on a life of their own. I've seen it happen plenty of times."

Slocum didn't doubt that for an instant. He'd seen rumors start off as pebbles that quickly grew into boulders once they got rolling. He was just grateful that a bothersome thing such as that could actually work in his favor for a change. As much as he would have liked to stand back and congratulate himself for getting Dawson's men interested enough to solve the murder that Wendell had tried to pin on him, Slocum had one more thing to do. "You need to tell the sheriff," he said in a voice that was muffled by the bandanna. Even though he'd never met Wendell, Slocum put a bit more gruffness into his tone to disguise himself even more.

Turning toward him as if Slocum had appeared out of thin air, Wendell said, "I thought that one was mute. First words he chooses ain't exactly ones I like."

"But they're ones you need to hear," Sanchez said. "He's

right. Mr. Dawson doesn't want to be connected to something like this."

"He's connected to a whole lot worse," Wendell
pointed out.

"Speculations and rumor," the Mexican replied. "Besides,
the ones doing the speculating aren't running to the law. If
this eventually gets back to the sheriff, he'll want to go running to Mescaline and have a word with Mr. Dawson. Even
if it's a small matter of asking a few questions, we don't want
anything to happen that might spook our friends from the
railroad. You sort it out now and end it."

Sanchez moved toward the older man, snatched the cigar
from Wendell's hand, and held it so the embers at its tip were
close enough to cast a red glow onto Wendell's face. "You'll
go to the sheriff, admit what you done, and make certain
Mr. Dawson's name isn't being dragged through the mud. I
don't give a damn what you say about that whore you seem
to love, just make sure there's no doubt in that lawman's
head that *you* killed that stable hand for reasons that don't
involve Dawson or any of his men."

"I already lost an old friend," Wendell sighed. "Killed
him myself. Viv won't touch me again and neither will my
wife. That doesn't leave me with much else to lose."

"How about an eye?" Sanchez said as he moved the lit
cigar closer to that target. "How about both of them? How
about your fingers as that kid behind me whittles them down
like kindling? How about your business and your house
when my mute friend there burns them both to the ground?"

Slocum didn't like being included with a gang of bloodthirsty outlaws, but he doubted any of those threats would
come to fruition. There were already tears streaming down
Wendell's face and a quiver in his lips as he babbled, "All
right, all right. I'll tell the sheriff the truth. I never meant to
drag Mr. Dawson into anything. I don't even remember his
name coming up. I just wanted to hurt Derrick for taking
Viv away from me."

"Trust me," Slocum said. "A woman like that . . . she was never yours to begin with."

That truth hit Wendell like a load of bricks, leaving him empty and defeated. Even knowing what that same man had done to an innocent stable hand, Slocum couldn't help but pity the bastard.

18

Slocum watched from afar as Wendell made his confession on the front porch of Sheriff Marshal's house. The young lawman stood dumbfounded for most of the time, only lunging forward at the last minute to catch Wendell as he started to fall over. Propping Wendell onto his feet, the sheriff spotted the three men in the shadows and called out for some help. Sanchez led the other two as they turned away and walked off. The sheriff dragged Wendell inside. His prisoner was so overcome that he could barely move. He wouldn't be giving anyone any trouble.

The stable where they'd left their horses was in sight—a large blocky shadow in the distance. They walked along the back ends of a row of shops that were all closed up until morning. The night was so still that Slocum could hear a wind rustling when he stopped and turned to face the other two.

"No complaints from you," Sanchez said. "We ride out of here now and make camp outside of town. I know where we're going. Just follow close."

"And then what?" Slocum asked. "The three of you kill me and bury me in the desert?"

The Mexican's eyes narrowed as though he didn't need any light to see every pertinent detail in front of him. "Turning on us?" he scoffed. "I thought this would happen sooner."

"Did you think I'd trust any of you?" Slocum asked.

"And did you expect any of us to believe that John Slocum would just walk up and join with us? The great hero of Mescaline?"

"Is that what they call me? I'm flattered."

"You will live forever in those people's legends. That's what happens to all men who accomplish something and then die with their boots on."

"Doesn't have to end that way," Slocum pointed out.

"Right. You can come back with us to see what Mr. Dawson wants to do with you."

"No. I meant it doesn't have to end that way for you. Of course, men like you don't exactly become legends. They're not even missed when they don't come back after a ride in the middle of the night."

"You want to bet your life on that?" Sanchez growled.

He wasn't going to budge. Slocum could tell that much by the way the Mexican planted his feet, squared his shoulders, and flexed his fingers anxiously above his holstered pistols.

The youngest gunman was a bit tougher to read. Slim was anxious, which also made the kid almost impossible to predict. It seemed just as likely that he could be frozen in fear or try to fire a shot before anyone else.

Slocum watched Sanchez for any hint of movement.

There was none to be seen. Apparently, Dawson had chosen the Mexican because he was the best man suited to walk away from this very situation. Dawson had also tried stacking the deck so Slocum would be outnumbered three to one. But Slocum had already put a plan into place where that was concerned. If Vivienne was good for anything more than causing trouble among men, it was to even up those odds just a bit.

Both men stood less than three paces away from each other. Close enough to read the other's expression in the dark, yet too far to take a swing at each other. While Sanchez prepared to draw one or both of his pistols, Slocum charged at him as if he'd been fired from a cannon.

Slocum covered the distance between them in one and a half bounding strides. Sanchez cleared leather, but his target was now close enough to swat his gun arm to one side and slip in past the firearm and get to the man behind it. Slocum was now less than an inch in front of Sanchez and used his remaining momentum to drive his knee into the Mexican's stomach. Sanchez expelled a gust of air, emptying his lungs and causing his entire body to droop forward. Grabbing the wrist of Sanchez's gun hand, Slocum kept that pistol pointed to the ground as he jammed the barrel of his .44 into the other man's gut.

"Drop it," Slocum said as he struggled to maintain his grip on the other man's wrist.

Rather than spit any kind of response at him, Sanchez shifted his other arm to try and pull the second pistol from his double-rig gun belt. Slocum did his best to keep him from getting to the weapon, but couldn't do much from where he stood. Once he knew Sanchez had gotten to his other pistol, Slocum's only recourse was to push his .44 in even harder and pull his trigger.

The gun thumped once and then again, lifting Sanchez off his feet with each shot. Blood filled the air behind him in a thick mist and Sanchez's last breath escaped from his lips. Slocum let the Mexican drop so he could turn and face the youngest gunman. Slim stood with his gun in hand, but hadn't taken a shot yet because there was no way he could keep from hitting Sanchez in the process.

"Dawson wants you to kill me," Slocum said. "What are you waiting for?"

"I don't wanna die."

"Dawson wouldn't send some innocent kid on a ride like

this. I heard what that Mexican said when he was making threats to Wendell. He knew damn well you could torture and kill just as good as anyone else."

Slim had indeed been trying to play the part of an innocent. His eyes were wide and his hands shook. And yet somehow the hand with the gun in it never turned all the way from Slocum's vicinity. In the blink of an eye, Slim's entire countenance changed. His expression shifted into one of a murderous animal and his body angled sideways into a duelist's stance.

The kid brought his gun up and clenched his finger around his trigger. By that time, however, Slocum had already taken his shot. The .44 bucked against his palm, sending a single round through a portion of Slim's chest. Since the kid had been standing sideways, the grazing bullet spun him around to present his back to Slocum.

Without wasting another second, Slocum started racing toward the stable. The signal they'd agreed upon was a gunshot, which meant Mikey had just been alerted to the fact that there was trouble. When he heard the rustle of movement behind him, Slocum paused just long enough to take a look over his shoulder. Sure enough, Slim had turned around and was bringing his gun up again. Slocum fired one more shot, which punched a hole through the younger man's heart, and dropped him right then and there.

Slocum broke once more into a run. Even though the stable wasn't far away, it seemed to take him an hour to reach it. When he got to the back door, he almost knocked it off its hinges with a single well-placed kick. He charged into the stable, ready to open fire or dive for cover depending on what he found inside.

Mike stood with his gun belt in one hand and his britches in the other. One leg was stuck through the leg of his jeans and a panicked expression covered his face now that he'd gotten a look at who'd stormed into the stable. Vivienne lay in a bed of straw, buck naked and legs spread. Upon seeing

Slocum, she merely sat up and waited to see what would happen next.

"Funny," Slocum mused, "but I'm usually the one caught in this sort of predicament with a woman. Feels a whole lot better to be the one with all my clothes on."

"You're always sneaking up behind me," Mike said. "This time you had to wait for when I'm dipping my wick before you could get the drop on me."

"This isn't about you, Mike. I've got bigger fish to fry and you just happen to keep getting in my way."

Mike yanked the pistol from his holster and fired a shot as he dove toward one of the stalls.

Slocum dropped to one knee as the wild shot hissed by, extending an arm to sight along the top of the .44.

After crawling through the loose straw on the floor, Mike got behind a wooden partition and tucked his legs in close to his body. When no more shots were fired or words were thrown at him, he couldn't help but take a look to see if he could find a juicy target for his next bullet.

The instant Mike's head popped around the partition, Slocum put a bullet through it. Mike flopped over and twitched through his last motions before giving up the ghost. Slocum refilled the spent rounds from his pistol as he walked over to make sure the other man was down for good.

"I knew you'd come back," Vivienne said while climbing to her feet and rushing over to embrace him. She wrapped her arms around Slocum and pressed her naked body against him. "Seeing you fight to protect me that way . . . it was so exciting."

"Wasn't protecting you," he said while reaching down to scoop up Mike's gun belt and pistol. He then moved her aside and went to his horse. "Didn't think you needed it."

Despite being naked, Vivienne stomped over to Slocum and shoved past him as if she was armed to the teeth. "You're taking me with you!"

"No, I'm not."

"I did this for you," she snapped while pointing down at Mike. "You owe me!"

"You did this for yourself," Slocum replied. "Which is the same reason you've done everything else."

"I'll tell the law about the men you killed here."

Slocum took the reins to his gelding and led the horse toward the stable's large front doors. "Do what you like, since the law should be here any second. Won't make a difference since any of the men you intended on robbing are either dead, in chains, or headed in one of those directions. You want my advice? Pack your things and find another bunch of idiots to string along. The ones in this town are through with you."

Vivienne finally pressed the dress she'd picked up against the front of her body and stomped her foot. "I won't spend another day in a goddamn barn!"

Now that he was outside, Slocum climbed into his saddle. Figures were approaching from the sheriff's office, shouting back and forth to each other as they closed in on the stable. Turning toward Vivienne, Slocum said, "Seems to me, a barn is where you belong." He then snapped his reins and rode north.

The sheriff shouted up a storm and even fired a few shots his way, but couldn't do much more than watch as his shadowy target disappeared.

19

Slocum rode through the entire night. He'd paid close attention to the trail Sanchez had used to get to Davis Junction, which made retracing his path a hell of a lot easier. A bright, mostly full moon cast enough light for him to see the ground in front of him. Having ridden the trail so recently, Slocum knew most of the terrain looked worse than it truly was. More often than not, the path was surrounded by rocky slopes or partly covered by scrub. When it came to actual maneuvering, the vast majority of it was done on flat rock or level dirt. There was a reason that trail was favored by killers who moved at night. Now that he knew his way, Slocum had no trouble in getting back to Mescaline before dawn.

He could feel the air beginning to warm, but the sun's rays were only just making themselves known when he was close enough to town to slow his horse. The minute his gelding's hooves stopped beating against the desert floor, Slocum heard more horses galloping toward him. He squinted toward town and quickly spotted a cloud of dust being kicked up on the western side. He counted two riders approaching. They were coming in such a hurry that he wouldn't have to wait long for them to arrive. Slocum reined his horse to a stop, hung his head low, and waited for them to reach him.

When they did, they each had a gun in hand. One man had a pistol and the other had a rifle propped against one hip so the barrel was pointed skyward. The one with the pistol approached Slocum while the other one hung back.

"That you, Sanchez?" the pistol man asked.

Slocum rocked in his saddle, keeping his head down so his hat kept his face from being seen. He muttered something in a voice that was scratchy enough to sound distressed and too low for any words to be clearly heard.

"What did you say?" the gunman asked. "You hurt?" After coming a bit closer, he asked, "That ain't Sanchez. Where's the others? That you, kid?"

Now that the man was close enough, Slocum lifted his head and gave him a good look at the face that had previously been hidden. He didn't recognize the gunman, but the man with the pistol seemed to know Slocum well enough. He spat out half a curse and brought his pistol up. Slocum already had a gun in each hand, both of which had been hidden beneath the coat that was wrapped around him. Like a bird of prey spreading its wings, Slocum extended both arms to take aim. He fired one shot point-blank into the closest man's chest, sparking a small fire on the gunman's shirt as the .44 sent a bullet through his heart. The gun in Slocum's left hand was Mike's, and he was close enough to his target to hit the man with the rifle.

The rifleman grunted and pitched backward to fall from his saddle. Slocum tucked Mike's gun away before riding over to check on him. Although he'd hit the rifleman, Slocum had been firing with his left hand, which meant he'd been lucky to hit him at all. The bullet had caught the rifleman in the shoulder, so Slocum finished him off with a shot from the .44 before snapping his reins and riding into town.

The top floor of the Three Star was already awake and, judging by the lights flickering in the windows and shadows moving about, had been for some time. Although the streets were nearly as deserted as the first time he'd walked down them, Slocum saw a pair of men standing outside the back entrance to the hotel. They were heeled, but hadn't skinned their guns just yet. Slocum watched them for a few seconds from the shadow of an alley, circled around to the other side of the building, and then knocked lightly on the wall.

When the first man rounded the corner, Slocum greeted him by stepping out from where he'd been hiding to place the blade of his boot knife against the gunman's throat.

"Dawson has you go out in twos now, does he?" Slocum whispered. "Call to your partner."

The gunman glared defiantly at him without making a sound.

Pressing the blade up into the man's neck while giving it just enough of a twist to draw blood, Slocum said, "Call out or you'll never make another sound again."

"Hector!" the gunman said. "Get over here."

Slocum listened for the sound of approaching footsteps. When they got close to rounding the corner, he pulled the knife away from the gunman's throat and followed up with a swift elbow delivered to his jaw. By the time that man fell over, Slocum was already pouncing on the one responding to the call. Hector barely had a chance to blink before he was grabbed and thrown face first against the wall.

Hector reached for his gun, but that hand was slapped aside and he was given another taste of the hotel's exterior.

When Hector tried to turn around, he was held in place by an arm that encircled his neck from behind. He tried to speak, but Slocum squelched those words by applying more pressure. After a few more seconds, Hector's body went limp.

Hunkering down beside the unconscious men, Slocum dug through their pockets until he found a ring of keys in one of them. There were only three keys on the ring, and he only needed to try two of them before the back door of the hotel opened. Slocum stepped inside to find himself in a kitchen, where two women worked to prepare breakfast while a burly man in a sweat-soaked shirt watched over them.

"Who . . ." the man asked. He must have put the pieces together quickly enough because he went for his gun as Slocum shut the door.

Fortunately, there were plenty of heavy objects about. Slocum grabbed one of them, a small iron skillet, and threw it. The big man had his pistol most of the way from its holster when the skillet knocked into the side of his head with a dull clang. He staggered sideways, blood streaming from his head, and slid to the floor.

Slocum calmly approached him, took the man's pistol, and then told the women, "Keep an eye on him. If he starts to wake up, give him another taste of that skillet." After adding the pistol to the growing collection under his belt, Slocum asked, "He's one of Dawson's men, right?"

One of the women nodded.

"Good. Are there any more nearby?"

"T-Two just outside. Where you came from."

"Thanks," Slocum said. "What's behind that door?"

The woman who hadn't found her voice yet looked at the narrow door and replied, "Stairs to the second and third floor."

"Are all of Dawson's men on the third floor?"

Both women nodded. "Hotel guests on the second."

"Good. Stay here and keep your heads down."

Slocum pulled the door open and worked his way up the narrow stairs as quickly and quietly as he could. His .44 was in hand, and the other guns he'd collected were tucked under his gun belt, where he could easily get to them. Once he reached the top of the dark staircase, he opened the door a crack to take a look at who was in the hallway. All but one of the doors were closed. One man stood at the top of the stairs at the far end of the hall. Another walked slowly back to one of the rooms.

Slocum watched the man closest to him approach one of the closed doors and start digging into his pocket for something. The man wore a gun belt, but was less concerned with the hog leg strapped to his side than he was in trying to find whatever was eluding his probing hand. Slocum's first thought had been to let that man get into his room, but the longer he fidgeted at that door, the likelier it became that more gunmen would show themselves. Once the man at the door seemed flustered enough, Slocum exploded from the cramped little staircase and walked straight at him.

The man barely seemed to notice at first. Having someone emerge from that stairwell couldn't have been too uncommon. He took a second glance, however, recognized Slocum's face, and reached for his pistol. By that time, Slocum had driven a solid punch into his stomach and followed up by grabbing a handful of hair and slamming the man's face into the door he'd been unable to open.

The man near the staircase saw what happened and went for his gun. Rather than do anything as sensible as run for cover, Slocum stormed straight down the hall while drawing his .44. Both of them fired quick shots and both bullets wound up buried in a wall without harming anyone. Slocum's, however, was close enough to its mark to whip past the other man's head and send him reflexively backward.

Slocum quickened his pace down the hall, swinging the .44 like a club and connecting with the other man's wrist. The man dropped his pistol and let out a nervous wail as his foot slipped on the edge of the top stair. Slocum grabbed the front of the man's shirt, shoved him onto the banister, and angled him toward the stairs.

The man's wail turned into a frightened cry as he started

to fall down the stairs. Slocum kept him from toppling, maintaining a hold on him while moving down the stairs and dragging the man along for the ride. After holstering the .44, Slocum used both hands to shove the man all the way down to the second floor.

Somewhere along the way, the man got his balance, but was unable to regain control of his descent. His boots slipped and skidded over every other stair as Slocum continued to shove him downward. When they finally reached the first-floor landing, Slocum pivoted on both feet and tossed the man through the hotel's front window.

The gunman's back hit the glass first and the rest of his body followed. After staggering down two floors and being tossed with all the strength Slocum could muster, he broke through the window to land on the boardwalk outside. Ignoring the astonished expressions on the faces of people in the lobby and dining room, Slocum strutted through the front door and stood over the man. Apart from plenty of cuts and gashes from the glass, the man would live. He wouldn't get up anytime soon, but he would live.

"All right, Dawson!" Slocum shouted up toward the third floor. "This is what you were so afraid of! Let's get it over with!"

The streets were empty, and the only sound to come from the hotel was the tinkling crash of smaller shards of glass falling to their death from the front window frame.

"Since all of your men seemed so surprised to see me," Slocum added, "I'd say none of you expected me to leave the desert alive."

One of the third-floor windows slid up and Dawson stuck his head out. "Where are my men? What did you do to them?"

"I defended myself," Slocum replied. "They meant to kill me. Wasn't that what you told them to do?"

Baring his teeth in a sneer, Dawson pulled his head back inside and shut the window.

Slocum stood his ground, hoping that Ed's figures had been right where Dawson's men were concerned. If they were, that meant there weren't more than two or three more gunmen left apart from Dawson himself. Slocum did hear some movement on all sides, but it did not come from killers or assassins looking to do him in. There were windows and doors opening in all the surrounding buildings. Folks up and down the street watched from their vantage points to see what would happen next.

Eventually, heavy steps thumped from within the hotel. Abel Dawson came down the stairs, peered out through the broken front window at the man who still lay on the boardwalk, and then walked over to step through the door. Pointing down at the man with the little pieces of glass stuck throughout his body, Dawson said, "You dare call me out and make accusations when you kill my men right out in the open for all to see?"

"They're hired guns and murderers," Slocum said. "And they're not all dead. Some of them will live to see another day. That's more than what can be said about the friends and family of good people like Old Man Garrett."

"That old man overstepped his bounds," Dawson replied. "Just like you did! You never should have come back to this town, Slocum. You got lucky once. It won't happen again."

"Brave talk from a man who doesn't have anyone to back him up."

Dawson smiled broadly and stood with his hands propped upon his hips. "Don't need anyone to back me up. I'm the mayor. Duly appointed and elected. That makes me untouchable. You're just a killer, John. A quick gun hand and no conscience. You're the animal around here. Not me. What do you hope to accomplish anyway? You gonna gun me down in the street?"

Shaking his head, Slocum said, "The only reason you have any power around here is because you have a hold on these people. And the only thing that gives you that hold is your bunch of killers who will harm innocent women and children just to keep the town in line. I brought you out here to prove that you don't have any of those killers around you anymore."

"Is that so?" Dawson snapped his fingers and pointed at the door. "Tate, come on out here and escort this man to a jail cell."

Tate filled the doorway with a frame that was at least six and a half feet tall. Layer upon layer of muscle hung on him like several thick coats piled onto his shoulders, making him look more like a bear than a man. His hands were so thick that the shotgun he carried could very well have been a broomstick.

"And if Tate's not good enough for you, I've got plenty more," Dawson announced.

Slocum looked up and grinned. "The only other men I can see are the two who met me when I came to town." Waving to Matt and Luke, who watched from a third-floor window, he added, "And I sent them crying back to you."

Dawson's upper lip curled away from his teeth and he stuck out a thick finger to point at Slocum as he stomped forward. "Listen here, you! I'm the mayor of this town and there ain't a damn thing you or anyone else can do abou—"

A single rifle shot cracked through the air.

That was followed by another . . . and then a third. As more shots cracked through the air, they became impossible to count.

Several of them hit Dawson, sending him reeling backward to bounce against the Three Star's front door. When the shots finally became nothing more than an echo, Slocum turned around with gun drawn. What he found was a street that was quickly filling up with people. They were shopkeepers, bartenders, restaurant owners, all manner of folks who kept Mescaline up and running.

One of the men who stepped forward had a face that was familiar to Slocum, but not enough so that he could remember his name. He carried a rifle in his hands. "Thank you, Mr. Slocum," the man said.

"Who are you?" Slocum asked. "What did you just do?"

"I'm Bill Rose. Mr. Garrett's grandson."

A second man stepped forward, also carrying a rifle. "I'm Saul Adler," he announced. "We heard from Miss Redlinger and Ed Leigensheim that we were to be ready to back your play."

"You sure did that," Slocum said gratefully.

Adler shook his head solemnly. "What we did here today was something we should have done before things got so bad. I was head of the committee to make certain he didn't become mayor. The night after our first meeting, my wife was . . . defiled. That piece of scum laying there," he said while staring down at Dawson, "promised it would happen again . . . and again . . . unless I backed down. I love my wife, but we shouldn't have backed down."

"He had gunmen backing him up," Slocum said. "He was a killer."

"You took those gunmen away," Bill said. "And you made it impossible for us to deny what he was. We may have not been out where you could see us all the time, but we were watching. Listening. This was the first time Dawson has poked his nose out of that hotel without being surrounded by hired guns. We appreciate what you did, Mr. Slocum. Appreciate what you were going to do . . . but it was our responsibility to put that bastard down."

Slocum nodded. Looking over to Tate, he asked, "What's your next move, big fellow?"

Tate gently set his shotgun down and said, "I'll gather my things and be gone."

"There's still a few more inside," Slocum told Adler.

"We can handle Matt and Luke."

Holstering his gun, Slocum said, "Yeah. I think you have everything well in hand. If anyone comes around asking for me, tell them I'm long gone."

"Anything you say, Mr. Slocum."

Folks drifted out into the street wearing grateful smiles and looking around at Mescaline as if they hadn't seen it in years. They waved at Slocum and wished him well as he made his way toward Anna Redlinger's house. There was still some important business to settle before putting Mescaline behind him one last time.